MYSTERIES IN OUR NATIONAL PARKS

MYSTERY
#7

OVER THE EDGE

GLORIA SKURZYNSKI AND ALANE FERGUSON

NATIONAL GEOGRAPHIC SOCIETY

WASHINGTON, D.C.

To Marcel Damgaard,

a young man of intelligence,

character, and charm who touched our lives.

Text copyright © 2002 Gloria Skurzynski and Alane Ferguson

Cover illustration copyright © 2002 Loren Long

Map by Carl Mehler, Director of Maps;
Map research and production by Gregory Ugiansky and Martin S. Walz

This is a work of fiction. Any resemblance to living persons or events other than descriptions of natural phenomena is purely coincidental.

Library of Congress Cataloging-in-Publication Data
Skurzynski, Gloria.
  Over the edge / by Gloria Skurzynski and Alane Ferguson.
  — (Mysteries in our national parks ; #7)
Summary: While she studies condors in the Grand Canyon a scientist's life is threatened, and the strange, hostile, teenage computer whiz in her family's foster care might be involved.
  ISBN 0-7922-6677-3 (Hardcover)
  ISBN 0-7922-6686-2 (Paperback.)
  [1. Condors—Fiction. 2. Endangered species—Fiction. 3. Grand Canyon National Park (Ariz.)—Fiction. 4. Internet—Fiction. 5. Foster home care—Fiction. 6. Arizona—Fiction. 7. National parks and reserves—Fiction. 8. Mystery and detective stories.]
  I. Ferguson, Alane. II. Title. III. Series.
  PZ7.S6287 Ov 2002
  [Fic]—dc21
                                2001003191

Printed in the United States of America

ACKNOWLEDGMENTS

The authors want to offer a very special and warm thanks to Pam Cox, Park Interpretive Ranger at Grand Canyon's inner canyon, who helped us immeasurably. Our sincere thanks go also to Elaine Leslie and R.V. Ward, Wildlife Biologists; Rex Tilousi of the Havasupai Tribe; Mike McGinnis, Law Enforcement Ranger; Sandra Perl, Grand Canyon Public Affairs; Shawn Farry and Bill Heinrich of The Peregrine Fund (www.peregrinefund.org); Phillip B. Danielson, Ph.D., Department of Biological Sciences, University of Denver; and to the Greater Los Angeles Zoo Association.

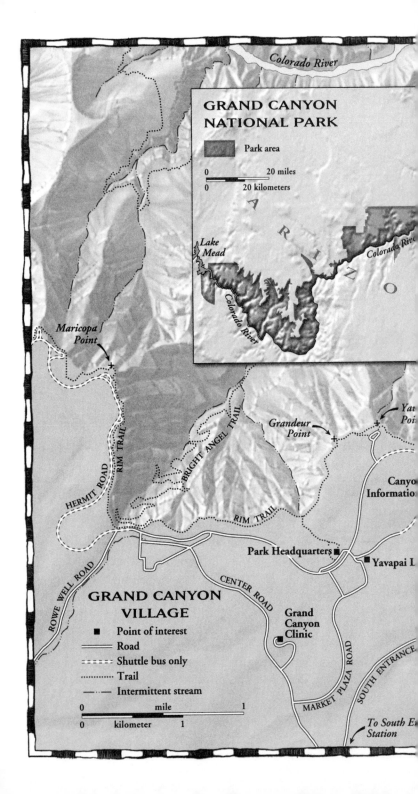

Colorado River

GRAND CANYON
NATIONAL PARK

Park area

0   20 miles
0   20 kilometers

A R I Z O

Lake
Mead

Colorado River

Colorado River

Maricopa
Point

RIM TRAIL

BRIGHT ANGEL TRAIL

Grandeur
Point

Yav
Poi

HERMIT ROAD

RIM TRAIL

Canyo
Informatio

Park Headquarters ■

■ Yavapai I

ROWE WELL ROAD

CENTER ROAD

GRAND CANYON
VILLAGE

■   Point of interest
——   Road
-----   Shuttle bus only
··········   Trail
—·—·   Intermittent stream

0   mile   1
0   kilometer   1

Grand
Canyon
Clinic

MARKET PLAZA ROAD

SOUTH ENTRANCE

To South E
Station

UNITED STATES

ARIZONA

The Peregrine Fund
Field Office

Colorado River

Vermilion Cliffs

Area
Enlarged
Below

Tusayan

Area
Enlarged
at Left

ARIZONA

Mather Point

RIM TRAIL

DESERT VIEW DRIVE

N

PARK DATA

State: Arizona

Established as a National Park: 1919

Area: 1.2 million acres, including 277 miles of the Colorado River

Climate: South Rim summer temperatures range from the 50s to the 80s (degrees F); the North Rim is normally 10° cooler due to its higher elevation; the canyon floor is about 35° hotter.

Natural Features: Multicolored layers of limestone, sandstone, and shale, formed by a succession of ancient seas, deserts, and marshes, make up the walls of a mile-deep, 10-mile wide canyon sculpted by the Colorado River over the past five to six million years.

ow October sun turned the massive stone walls blood red. From behind the rim of the canyon he stared at her, rage building in his throat until it almost choked him. She wanted to steal away his freedom. People like her were always trying to force their will on others, but he would stop her, and in a way that would stop them all. He searched along the nearby piñon trees, but they were empty. No one was watching except a raven circling on unseen currents of air. You won't tell, will you, he silently asked the bird. The raven screeched in reply. It was a sign. Now was the time.

She'd moved even closer to the rim. One push, he knew, would send her over the edge.

CHAPTER ONE

In his dream, Jack heard something ringing. Groggy, he reached out to hit the snooze button on his alarm clock. Was it really time to get up, or could he squeeze in just a few extra minutes of sleep? He buried his head into his pillow, arguing with himself about whether to climb out of bed immediately or wait for the alarm to go off the next time. Yes or no? Sleep for five more minutes, or roll out now, just to make sure he'd packed all the right camera equipment for the trip to the Grand Canyon? Eyes closed, he slipped back into the dream where he soared within the cavernous Grand Canyon, past fern-decked alcoves and springs that burst from the rock like fountains of gems. Beneath him the Colorado River unfurled in a ribbon of silver, winding between walls of orange-red rock....

Ringing jarred him once more, and he raised his

head, puzzled. The snooze button shouldn't have gone off again that fast. He opened one eye to look at the clock. Two-seventeen in the morning! It wasn't his alarm clock he'd been hearing, but the doorbell.

"Come in, come in," he heard his mother say, while a familiar voice answered, "I really hate to wake you, Olivia, but it's an emergency."

"Wait—let me get Steven."

Jack hurriedly pulled on a pair of sweatpants. He reached the living room just as his father got there and heard Ms. Lopez say, "Hello, Steven. Oh, I'm so sorry— I've wakened Jack and Ashley, too." Jack's 11-year-old sister had stumbled into the living room, rubbing her eyes with her palms. Dark, curly hair swirled around her head, and her flannel horse-print pajamas seemed too big for her small frame. Although Ashley was 11, she wasn't much taller than a 9-year-old. Jack, who was two years older, stood a full foot taller.

"I really do apologize," Ms. Lopez said hurriedly. "It's just that this whole situation has blown up into quite a mess. I've got a young man who is in some serious trouble. He needs to get out of Wyoming—fast."

"S'OK," Jack mumbled as his father asked, "What's going on?"

All four of the Landons were used to Ms. Lopez's unexpected visits, but none had ever been in the middle of the night. A social worker who placed temporary-care foster children into safe houses, Ms. Lopez had always been dedicated to the children thrust into her care. Her kids were the ones who needed shelter for short periods until their problems could be worked out, troubled children who seemed to hover at the edge of upheaval. Over the past year, the Landons had provided shelter for half a dozen kids who needed help. Now it looked as though another one was about to come into their lives in the dark stillness of this mid-October night.

Motioning to the figure behind her, she said, "This is Morgan Rogers. He's a computer whiz from Dry Creek."

"Hi," Ashley and Jack said, while their parents smiled and added, "Nice to meet you."

A tall, thin, hollow-chested boy who wore his dark hair in a ponytail, Morgan stood rooted to the entryway floor. A few straggly whiskers of a not-quite-grown goatee curled around his chin like smoke, smudging skin so pale it seemed he'd never walked in daylight. His brown eyes, though, had a snap to them, hinting at sparks beneath.

"Morgan, remember what I talked to you about on the way here?" Ms. Lopez prompted. "Say hello to the Landons."

"Oh, yeah. I'm supposed to learn to conform to society's standards, even if I believe they're for everyone else and not me," he said as he gave a mock bow.

Sighing, Ms. Lopez shook her head. "Anyway, to continue—the other day, Olivia, you told me you'd be going to the Grand Canyon."

"Yes, I've been called to help with the condors."

"That's what I thought. I realize this is terribly short notice." She hesitated, then said, "I might as well just come right out and ask. Do you think there is any possible way that you could take Morgan with you?"

"But we're leaving first thing in the morning!" Olivia protested. "I can't see how—"

"I know, I know. I truly hate to put you on the spot like this. When you learn what's happening to this boy, I think you'll agree it's an extraordinary situation."

"Go on," Jack's father said.

Ms. Lopez rushed ahead, "Not that he's completely innocent in all of this—"

"Who says I'm guilty?" Morgan countered, an expression Jack couldn't quite read curling the edge of his lip. "Hey, I investigated the law before I started, and I'm telling you those intellectual pygmies will *never* make it stick! The problem is that the whole town's filled with freaking morons. There's not a person in Dry Creek who even knows how to *spell* First Amendment, let alone—"

"Morgan—be—quiet!" Ms. Lopez shot each syllable into the air in a way that made Ashley jump and Morgan clamp his mouth tight. In all the time he'd known Ms. Lopez, Jack had never once heard her raise her voice, but now he watched as she planted her round, five-foot-three-inch frame directly in front of Morgan, who stared back at her with an inscrutable expression.

"Young man, I want you to consider that the people in this room—the Landons—are the ones who can keep you out of juvenile detention. They are your only chance. Do you understand what I am saying to you?"

"Yeah," Morgan answered. "You're telling me to keep my mouth shut."

Ms. Lopez nodded.

"That's censorship."

"No, that's wisdom. Look, I'm already out on a limb here. Don't cut it out from under me. If I fall, so do you." The room was suddenly so quiet that Jack could hear the hum of the kitchen refrigerator droning a long, drawn-out note against the living room clock's rhythmic ticking. Olivia shifted uncomfortably while Ms. Lopez kept Morgan locked in an unflinching gaze. When Ashley's eyes met Jack's, questions passed between them. What had Morgan done that would send him to detention? Was he dangerous?

Steven cleared his throat loudly. "Well, why don't we all sit down," he said, sweeping his arm toward the couch. "You can fill us in on what this is about. Before we get started, would anyone like a glass of water? Or soda?"

"No, thank you," Ms. Lopez said, while Morgan just shook his head. In an odd way, mentioning something as common as a drink seemed to break the tension. The two made their way to the couch and sank into the plump cushions, while Olivia and Steven took the remaining chairs. Ms. Lopez unbuttoned her gray wool coat as Morgan unzipped his parka. Jack and Ashley dropped to the floor, legs crossed, watching expectantly.

"All right. I'm sure you have a thousand questions. Let me start with the incident itself," Ms. Lopez began. "As I mentioned, Morgan lives in the little town of Dry Creek, Wyoming, about 70 miles from Jackson Hole."

"Yes, I know where it is," Steven said.

"Well, if you've seen it, Steven, you know it's a ranch town, small, quiet, and…traditional."

"Populated by a bunch of lemmings," Morgan broke in scornfully. "My mom and dad got scared of the big city of San Francisco—that's where we used to live— and decided we'd all get back to basics in the cow town of Dry Creek. I didn't want to go, but hey, I'm only a minor. I have zero rights." He made an O shape with his thumb and index finger and punched it into the air. "I found out fast that the only way to fit into Cow Town was to turn into another stupid lemming. I refused. That's why they're after me."

A frown passed over Olivia's face. "After you?"

"Yeah," Morgan answered coolly. "They're after me, all right. I'm a man on the run."

Except for his hair and his black shirt and jeans, everything about Morgan was pale. His skin looked translucent, like wax, while his fingers seemed long and white like bones. Jack could imagine how a kid like Morgan would stick out in a town like Dry Creek.

"Morgan, you're not helping. Why don't you hold on and let me explain to them why you're here," Ms. Lopez urged.

Throwing his back into the sofa, Morgan squeezed his eyes shut. "You're right, I shouldn't talk, even though I *am* the principal player."

Ms. Lopez went on, trying, it seemed, to ignore him. "As Morgan said, he didn't exactly fit into Dry Creek. There was some…trouble."

"Trouble?" Olivia asked. "What kind of trouble?"

"Unpleasant things were said and done to Morgan in the high school. In retaliation, he created a Web site to deal with his feelings. He…he wrote about the townspeople. In less than flattering terms."

Steven's pale brows crunched together. "What does making a Web site have to do with getting Morgan out of town?"

"You've got to understand, this was a pretty strong Web site. Morgan wrote about his principal, his teachers, and a lot of the students who'd given him a hard time."

With his eyes still closed, Morgan muttered, "So? Everything I wrote was true. Armed only with facts, I flamed Cow Town!"

"Which of course made the people of Dry Creek hopping mad," Ms. Lopez rushed on. "Look, I can understand their anger, but not what happened next. The sheriff got a warrant and broke into Morgan's house. Deputies confiscated his computer and placed

Morgan—who is only 15 years old—under arrest."

"Arrest? For what?" Olivia sounded alarmed.

"For slandering the townspeople. It got so out-of-hand the deputies decided Morgan had to leave town and stay in detention in Jackson Hole. That's no place for a kid like Morgan, Olivia. They'll eat him alive in there! If he leaves with you, I buy time to fight this thing."

His voice grim, Steven said, ""Detention can be pretty rough."

"Exactly. It should be the very last resort." For a moment, Ms. Lopez seemed to look past them, as though she were picturing a space totally different from the one she was in, a place where windows were barred and doors were locked. "You know, in my job, I see a lot of hardened souls," she said softly. "But that's not Morgan. No matter how wrong he was, he never threatened anyone. Being obnoxious should not be a crime."

Steven nodded, while Olivia looked less certain. Jack knew his mother, knew how she demanded that everyone in the Landon family show respect for others. Morgan did sound as though he had a first-class attitude, and yet Jack couldn't help being intrigued by a kid who would unapologetically break rules, going so far as to use his own Web site for an in-your-face payback. Ever since he could remember, Jack had always colored between life's lines, pretty much doing what his parents told him to do while racking up rows of straight A's next to a rainbow of merit badges. How would it be to have real enemies? How would it be to do exactly what you wanted, no matter what?

Morgan scowled deeply. "I just hope those idiot bozos in the crime lab don't start messing with my computer and screw it up."

This time there was no mistaking Olivia Landon's reaction. She sat back in her chair stiffly, asking, "Crime lab? Why would they take your computer to a crime lab?"

"I've been charged with criminal libel. They took my computer as evidence. Aren't you tracking this?"

For a moment it looked as though Olivia were going to reply, but then she thought better of it. Ashley whispered into Jack's ear, "What a jerk!"

After a quick glance at her watch, Ms. Lopez rose to her feet, telling Morgan to come with her as she made her way to the front door. "So now you know the situation," she said, shrugging her coat back onto her shoulders. "I realize it's a lot to throw at you all at once, so here's what I'm going to do. I'll take Morgan back to my car while the four of you talk. Olivia, I don't want you to feel pressured here. If it doesn't work out, I'll understand. Just open the door when you have your answer, and we'll take it from there."

Morgan shoved his hands deep into his pockets and followed her through the front door, which shut softly behind them. The four Landons sat staring at one another, unsure, it seemed, as to what to do next. Olivia was the first to speak.

"I feel bad about his situation, but I don't see how we can possibly take him with us. First of all, there's the problem of an airline ticket and his clothing...."

"Don't worry about the details. We can make it all work," Steven replied.

Nodding slowly, Olivia paused before going on. "I guess I'm uncomfortable accepting someone who's been involved in a crime. I don't like his attitude. He doesn't even seem sorry for what he did."

"Wait a minute. Are you serious?" Steven jerked his fingers through his hair, which caused it to stand up in blonde tufts. "OK, OK, Morgan wrote a couple nasty comments on his own computer. Slap him on the wrist, and tell him he's a bad boy. But mouthing off on a computer is not a real crime."

"Steven, *libel* is a crime."

"Not in this case. And not when you're 15! You don't know what detention is like," he said, his voice heating up. "Remember—I was bounced from one foster home to another when I was a boy. One time they ran out of places to put me, so I had to stay in detention. Trust me, that kid does not belong there. If we can help him, we should."

"I think he's mean," Ashley declared.

"Nobody asked what you think," Jack shot back. "Dad's right. We ought to do what we can to help."

Olivia leaned forward, gently smoothing the top of Ashley's tangled head. Then she looked into Jack's eyes, hers brown, his gray-blue. "Why don't you and Ashley head back to bed, OK?"

It wasn't what she said, but the way she said it that let Jack know there was no use arguing. Reluctantly pulling himself to his feet, he shuffled as slowly as possible to his room, straining to hear as his parents' voices rose and fell, his mother's calm, his father's urgent.

"Jack, wait a second," Ashley whispered.

Sighing, he leaned against his door frame and looked down at his sister. "What?"

"You know how I sometimes get feelings about things, and then they come true? Well, I have a feeling about Morgan. It's a really, really *bad* feeling, Jack."

It was cold in the hallway, especially with just a T-shirt on for a top. "I don't have time for this," Jack groaned. "It's probably the burritos you had for dinner."

"I mean it, Jack."

"So do I. Eat a Tums or something. Good night."

He left her standing there. Wrapping himself into his plaid comforter, he watched as the red, boxy numbers on his alarm clock blinked away the minutes. Determined to wait for the verdict, Jack willed himself to stay awake, until a buzzing startled him and his eyes flew open to morning light shining though his window blinds and a small figure hovering in his doorway.

"Morgan—is he here?" Jack mumbled.

Ashley nodded, then walked away.

CHAPTER TWO

During the first part of their flight from Jackson Hole, Morgan told Jack a little about his school, complaining that Dry Creek was populated by redneck kids with low-octane brains. In the small town of 700, there was nothing to do but ride horses, which Morgan adamantly refused to do, and nothing to see except scrawny cows and scrawnier chickens. Every other comment he made was punctuated by his request to use Olivia's laptop, which Olivia declined to hand over. Morgan kept talking, but when the seat-belt light blinked off, Ashley quickly escaped toward the rest room. Jack followed.

"I don't think I can take another two hours listening to him," she complained the minute they were out of Morgan's hearing. "He is driving me absolutely crazy."

They bumped their way down the narrow aisle until they reached the back of the plane. A man with a bald, round head and a much rounder paunch stood ahead of them, shifting from foot to foot as he waited for the tiny "Occupied" sign to slide to "Vacant." For a moment, Jack wondered how the man would fit into a bathroom as small as a metal coffin, but when the door open, the man managed to turn sideways and squeeze inside.

"I mean, all he does is talk about himself," Ashley continued. "Have you noticed that everyone else is stupid, and he's brilliant, and blah, blah, blah. When Mom told him about going to the Grand Canyon because the condors were dying, he just stared out the window like he didn't even care. Maybe if everyone hates him, he should get a clue. I want to say, 'Hello— the problem is *you*, Morgan.'"

"He's not so bad," Jack said defensively.

When Ashley gave him a look, he said, "OK, he's weird, but he's also…interesting."

"As long as you buy into everything he's saying. And he's like *obsessed* with computers. Mom thinks he could be dangerous, and I think she's right."

"Oh, come on. When did Mom say that?" Jack demanded.

"Last night. While you were in bed, I snuck down the hall and listened in on their conversation. I've never heard them argue about taking in a foster kid before." With her fingers curled against her protruding hip, Ashley waved her free hand in the air, almost hitting a flight attendant who hustled by. "Finally, Mom told Dad if it was that important she'd go along, but she thought any kid vicious enough to trash a whole town had a lot of pent-up rage. Then Dad told her that it was a lot healthier to write about bad feelings than act on them, and then they called Ms. Lopez inside and took Morgan."

The lavatory door opened, and the round man pushed his way out. Ashley was next.

"What I can't figure out is why you even like him," she declared from the doorway. "He's a punk."

"I didn't say I liked him."

"You don't have to." With that, Ashley snapped the door shut, leaving Jack to think about what she'd said. It wasn't exactly that he liked Morgan, but he couldn't help being drawn to his…what was it? Maybe his self-assured view of the world according to Morgan. His braininess. Maybe even the fact that people thought him dangerous, although Jack didn't believe it. By the time Jack had made it back to his seat, he could tell Morgan had said something that had set Jack's mother off again. He could see her eyes flashing, while Ashley, already seated, wore an I-told-you-Morgan-was-trouble expression.

"Hey—what's going on?" he asked, settling down in his seat. He was in the middle, Morgan had folded himself in next to the window, and Ashley had the aisle. Their parents were seated directly opposite them.

"Morgan just informed us that he's not at all inter-ested in the Grand Canyon," Olivia answered tartly. "He says it's nothing more than a big hole in the ground."

Jack pressed his fingertips into his forehead.

"What do you expect from an anarchist? The definition of my personality is to rebel. If the masses like it, I won't," Morgan answered.

"I'm sure you'll change your mind when you see the canyon," Steven commented, trying to smooth things. "Olivia, why don't you tell me more about your plan for the condors? What's your first move?"

Twisting back into her seat, Olivia allowed herself to get drawn into a conversation about the enormous, prehistoric birds that were dying in the Grand Canyon. Jack let out a breath. The immediate danger had passed.

"What was that all about?" Jack hissed at Morgan.

"You mean just now? Nothing. I was just disagreeing."

"Did you have to be rude?"

"Hey, it's free speech."

"It's stupid. You can't say everything that pops into your mind. Besides, this is my family. You get my mom upset and the whole thing goes south. If you want to get along with *me*, you need to learn when to shut up!"

Morgan's defiance quickly changed to amusement and then settled into what might have been a glimmer of respect. "OK," he said, nodding. Keeping his voice low enough that the others couldn't hear, he whispered, "I guess it's true that every once in a while, I do cross the verbal line. I didn't think calling the Grand Canyon a hole in the ground was that big a deal, but I stand corrected."

"One more thing," Jack said pointedly, "Why don't you at least *ask* my mom about the condors?"

Morgan's thin brows met. "Condors?"

"Yeah. The condors. You know, the reason we're going." Jack rotated his hand like a wheel, trying to get Morgan's mind clicking, but nothing seemed to register. "Remember, she talked about it while we were buying your airline ticket? Weren't you listening?" It seemed almost unbelievable that Morgan could have inhabited the same space as the Landons while they discussed the mystery of the condors and their strange deaths, and have blocked it out so completely.

"Tell me again," he said, stretching his legs under the seat in front of him.

"Ask my mom."

"No, I don't want her to know I wasn't tracking. So, what's the deal?"

"Well, like my mom said, the condors are very, very rare. Almost extinct. They used to nest all through the Southwest and the Grand Canyon during the Ice Age, but they disappeared at the end of the Ice Age. Are you listening?"

Morgan's lids had drifted shut, but he quickly snapped them open. "Yeah. I'm just thinking with my eyes closed."

"So then the condors made a comeback to the Southwest and the canyon at the same time the white settlers showed up. The settlers hunted and killed the condors. Now there are fewer than 200 of them in the whole world."

"Right. I remember that part. Aren't they giant vultures or something? Their wingspan is, like, nine feet wide. Yeah, they're these huge, extremely ugly birds that eat dead things."

Jack nodded. "Anyway, they're dying, and nobody knows how to stop it. So the people at the Grand Canyon called in my mom to help solve the mystery. She's a wildlife veterinarian, and my dad's a professional photographer.

"Uh-huh."

"It's life or death for these birds, Morgan. Ask my mom, and she'll tell you the whole thing. Say you want to know more about the condors, and the hole-in-the-ground stuff will be forgotten. Guaranteed."

"If I ask her about the birds, do you think she'll let me use her laptop?"

"No. Maybe. Probably not." Sighing, Jack said, "Here—take this," and handed over his own Game Boy and his new game called Alien Child. That did it. As soon as Morgan switched on the Game Boy, something inside him seemed to shut down. He didn't so much as look out the airplane window for the rest of the flight to Phoenix. He kept playing the game as they stood in line to rent a car and as they drove, grunting a reply when Steven told him they'd just entered Grand Canyon National Park. While the Landons strained to see even a shadow of what lay beyond the rim, Morgan concentrated on the Game Boy, its greenish light barely illuminating his face, his fingers deftly punching the tiny controls as his eyes stared, unblinking. Jack had never seen anyone so transfixed by something electronic. It was as if Morgan had fused himself into that tiny screen. He found himself agreeing with Ashley: Morgan really was strange.

#

"Get up, Jack. You said you wanted to see the sunrise hit the walls of the Grand Canyon. It's time to rise and shine!"

Jack felt a gentle tug on his covers, but he pulled them close and curled into their protective warmth. "Too early," he muttered to his mother.

Ignoring him, Olivia gave the edge of his bed a playful bounce. "Come on—up and at 'em! You too, Morgan. Throw on some clothes. You can shower when we get back. And Jack, don't forget your camera. I'm turning on the light right…now!"

"No—" Jack began, but there was a click and a flood of light stabbed his eyes. His mother stood, fully dressed in stonewashed jeans and a hooded jacket. Although wrinkles lined the corners of her eyes when she smiled, Olivia looked young and trim. And full of energy.

Morgan grabbed a pillow and put it over his face.

"What time is it?" he asked in a muffled voice.

"Six o'clock."

"Six?" The pillow flew off his face as he looked at her incredulously. "Six *a.m.?* No normal human being gets up this early. I'll stay here while you Earth people go and do whatever homage you tree-hugging types do. I'm a creature of the night. I don't do mornings."

"Nice try. We're doing this as a family, which now includes you."

"I don't wish to be included."

"I'm afraid it's not a matter of what you wish." Olivia's voice had an edge to it, although Morgan didn't know her well enough to hear it.

Flopping a long, thin arm over his eyes, Morgan looked as though he were trying to block out the light in addition to blocking out Olivia. "Look, I've already seen the Grand Canyon. Virtually. I got a view from the comfort of my own computer, which is the perfect way to experience it—no bugs or heat or fatigue. I don't need the real thing."

"Let me assure you that there is absolutely no comparison between the two. Reality will always trump the virtual world. Besides that, I'm not leaving until I see you're truly up." She stood over him, her arms planted on her hips, until Morgan gave a loud, long sigh.

"Zealot," he muttered.

"Guilty as charged. And just one more little thing. I want to ask you a favor."

"Now what?" Morgan asked, his voice squeaking. "I'm already denying my physical body its sleep. What more can I give up?"

Olivia hesitated for only a moment before saying, "I'd like you to leave the Game Boy here while we go to the rim."

"Aw, *man!*" Morgan exploded.

"I noticed that you do tend to get a bit—involved—with that thing. You need to experience the Grand Canyon with your whole being."

Pulling himself to a sitting position, Morgan swung his legs over the side of the bed. A large, white T-shirt hung on him like an oversize shroud, revealing how thin Morgan really was. Elbows protruded in knots from branch-like arms. His chest was sunken, as if he didn't have enough muscle to hold his body in anything but a pale question mark.

"I don't believe this! You're just like the people at Dry Creek. Why can't I have the freedom to experience the Grand Canyon in my own way?"

Olivia's lips pressed together before she finally answered, "Humor me. What do you say, Morgan? Will you leave the Game Boy?"

"Sure. Whatever," he answered.

Olivia looked both surprised and pleased. "Thank you. You won't be sorry. And now for you, my son," she began, turning her gaze on Jack. "I see you're still in bed. We'll miss the sunrise—"

"OK, OK, " Jack moaned. "Go back in your room so we can get dressed."

Stretching muscles that had stiffened from hours of travel, Jack waited for the door to shut behind Olivia. Once again, his parents were in an adjoining room with Ashley, while he and a foster kid—this time Morgan— shared the connecting space. The room at Yavapai Lodge looked clean and homey, but not fancy.

"It was nice of you to agree about the Game Boy, Morgan. How far did you get on the new game?"

"Man, I totally conquered it, but it's a game for eight-year-olds or computer cretins. I'm just using it as a crutch until I can get my hands on a real computer."

"There's some good stuff on Game Boy," Jack answered lamely, embarrassed that Morgan thought his games were childish.

"If you think that stuff is good, it's only because you don't know any better. Haven't you ever been on the Internet?"

"Sure. For school reports and stuff. I e-mailed a guy in Spain and a girl in Ireland for a class project."

"That means you, my man, need to see what a real game is all about." As Jack hurriedly pulled on his clothes Morgan kept talking, never pausing, as if he'd been charged with a new mission. "You get me your mother's laptop, and I'll show you graphics that'll blow your mind! There's a universe you've never experienced, an Internet cosmos where there are no rules, no boundaries. It's time you got out of your computer kindergarten and joined the cyberworld!"

"But, there's a lot of bad stuff on the Net. I don't want my mom's laptop to catch a virus or something."

Morgan quickly pushed his hair back off his face and trained his eyes on Jack. "Every year, people fall over the edge of the Grand Canyon. They die. You wouldn't want to miss seeing the scenery outside because there's an infinitesimal chance you could fall over the edge, right? It's the same with the Web—you factor in risk and go on." Sitting on the end of the bed, elbows drilling his knees, he said, "How would you like to see graphics so real they singe your hair, chat with your favorite rock star, or burn a disk of the hottest music for free?"

"Cool," Jack breathed.

"It's beyond cool. But you've got to grow up, my man. You go do the nature thing, and after you come back, I'll lead you into my world."

Jack could feel the roughness of the carpet beneath his feet as he pulled on his socks. "What do you mean? Aren't you coming?"

"I changed my mind. I never go anywhere I don't want to."

Morgan was interrupted by a knock on the door. "Behold the master!" Morgan said, dropping back onto his bed.

Steven called in, "You guys ready?"

As if by magic, Morgan's expression dissolved into one of distress as he lay back, his head drooping to one side. In a weak voice, he said, "Mr. Landon, can I talk to you?"

"Sure." Steven hurried inside, concern creasing his face. "Are you OK?"

"I feel like I'm going to puke. I think it's all the travel, not to mention the emotion, you know? I'm wiped. I need to stay here until my stomach calms down." A beat later, Morgan begged, "Please?"

Steven hesitated, glancing into his own room, then back to Morgan.

"Sure. Go ahead and rest. We'll be back in about an hour."

When the door closed, Morgan punched his fist triumphantly. "I rule!" he said.

All Jack could do was agree.

CHAPTER THREE

As they walked through the parking lot of Yavapai Point, Jack's thoughts turned from his guilt over letting Morgan manipulate his dad to pure anticipation of what lay ahead. The sky was lightening in the east, sending out delicate rays, burning the tips of the piñon pines until they looked as if they were on fire. The air itself seemed touched with gold. A walkway arced from the parking lot toward a small building; next to it were more pines, more slices of sky touching distant mountaintops, and yet, with less that a hundred yards to go, the view of the canyon itself eluded him.

"I can't believe we're this close, and we still can't see it," Ashley said, straining onto the tips of her toes. "I read that in some spots you can almost walk right to the edge before you realize you're on the rim."

Hoisting a backpack bristling with camera equipment onto his shoulders, Steven told her, "Just a little farther. We've got to go right past this building and then…."

He didn't finish his sentence. He didn't have to. In front of all of them loomed a vision that Jack could hardly believe, a vast space so incomprehensible it seemed to stretch across time itself. Golden-red rock descended in massive sheer-faced walls, ending in a tiny ribbon of water, a winding thread of silver that was the Colorado River. Shadows, ranging from brown to bluish-black, traced patterns against the enormous walls as if brushed by a painter's hand, the dark and light composing shapes that were alive and ever-changing and incomprehensibly beautiful. But it was the expanse between the canyon walls that took Jack's breath away. He was suddenly small, a tiny speck of matter on Earth, no bigger than a grain of sand and no more permanent than a snowflake. He stood with his family, perfectly still, taking in what he could in the silence. It was a good feeling, realizing where he fit. Everything seemed dwarfed here. He couldn't move his eyes from the enormity of the canyon, not even to take a picture.

"It's—it's…." Olivia stopped, shaking her head in wonder.

"I've seen pictures," Ashley whispered. "But they can't even begin to capture it. It's so much bigger. It's so much more beautiful."

Reverent, Steven said, "Nothing could capture this

canyon's spirit. I'm almost ashamed to even try putting it into photographs. The Native Americans called it Mountain Lying on its Back. It really is the mirror image of a mountain. Incredible."

"I wish we had hours to stand on this spot and drink in all this beauty," Olivia told them, "but I'm suppose to be at The Peregrine Fund field office at 10:00, and it's an hour-and-a-half drive. We need to get Morgan, grab a bite of breakfast, and take off."

"Where is the field office?" Jack asked.

"A place called Vermilion Cliffs. If all goes well, we might even get to see a condor!"

#

"There they are," Steven announced. "The Vermilion Cliffs. Wow, what a view! Let's stop for a minute so I can grab a few shots."

The second he pulled the rental car to a stop at the side of the two-lane highway, all four doors swung open and all four Landons jumped out, Steven and Olivia from the front, Jack and Ashley from the back. Morgan remained in the middle of the backseat, where he'd sat like a stone for the whole hour-and-a-half ride from the Grand Canyon. As an act of defiance, he'd brought the Game Boy, but if it bothered Olivia, she didn't let it show. She kept speaking to Morgan in a pleasant, brittle way that to Jack sounded strangely unlike his mother.

It was a tone she'd adopted after their encounter two hours earlier when the four Landons had returned from the Grand Canyon rim to Yavapai Lodge.

With the room's thick curtains drawn tight against the sun, Morgan had sat hunched over the Game Boy. He quickly looked up and said to Olivia, "You told me not to take it to the rim. You didn't say anything about not playing it here."

Dryly, Olivia said, "It seems your upset stomach has miraculously healed itself. That's fine, because we're going to get some breakfast and then start out for—"

"Oh no," Morgan said, clutching his middle. "I'm still too sick to go anywhere. I better talk to Mr. Landon."

Olivia shook her head. "That won't work this time. We're all going, including you. Grab your things."

And now, at the Vermilion Cliffs, Steven was attempting to draw Morgan out of the car, waving through the car window. "Hey, Morgan, wait'll you see this view of the cliffs! Come on, it's spectacular!"

"No thank you," Morgan answered as he deftly punched miniature Game Boy keys.

Olivia put her hand lightly on Steven's back, touching him where his shoulder blade protruded. "Leave him be," she said softly. "If he wants to ignore all this, he's only hurting himself."

"Exactly. That's why we shouldn't give up."

"I'm not giving up. I'm just not being taken in the way you seem to be."

"He's a troubled kid," Steven answered evenly, "but those are exactly the ones who need our help. It isn't like you to get rattled." He gave her a quick, sideways hug that tucked Olivia beneath his lanky arm. "Give him another chance—he'll warm up."

"I hope you're right," she murmured. "There's something about that boy that rubs me the wrong way."

"You worry about the condors, and I'll handle Morgan. Deal?"

"Deal," Olivia said.

Jack knew he'd better hurry if he was going to capture a perfect shot. The morning sun cast shadows that outlined every crevice in the mesa-topped range. Compared to the mile-high cliffs of the Grand Canyon, the Vermilion Cliffs were dwarfs, and the shape of them wasn't outstanding in this land of rugged peaks, pinnacles and crags, domes and forested ridges. But the colors! While other rock masses stood out in bold orange-reds, the reds of the Vermilion Cliffs had a bluish tinge. The blue-reds were layered, in horizontal stripes, by pale sedimentary rock left behind by ancient oceans. No wonder Native Americans called cliffs like these Land of the Sleeping Rainbow.

"Hey, where are the condors?" Ashley exclaimed, scanning the sky while shielding her eyes from the sun. "I thought you said they lived here."

"Ashley, it would be a minor miracle if you spotted a condor. Right now there's only one of them still out there in the wild. Come on, we've got to get to the field office." Olivia started the engine while Jack and Ashley piled once more into the backseat. Steven took the map and checked the route.

"Wait—I think this is it," Steven finally said. "The town of Vermilion Cliffs, christened after the cliffs of the same name."

Morgan, finally looking up, muttered, "This is supposed to be a *town?* Jeez, it's even smaller than Dry Creek! How many people live here?"

"About 30, I think," Olivia answered. "And 6 of them work for the condor program."

The town of Vermilion Cliffs consisted of a flat-roofed stone lodge with a neon "'Vacancy" sign flashing; a fly-fishing shop; a couple of little trailers; and around the back of a loop from the highway, a double trailer. They parked next to the double trailer. A placard identified it as The Peregrine Fund California Condor Project.

At the door, they were met by Shawn, the research project's chief biologist. Shawn had a beard that matched his hair, the same reddish brown they'd seen in their drive across the Painted Desert. Protective coloration, Jack thought, grinning to himself. Shawn would blend right in with the landscape. Tall and wiry, he must have been pretty tough—Olivia had said that every few days, Shawn strapped on a makeshift back-pack and hiked two miles to deliver 50-pound dead dairy calves to the hungry condors. When Olivia told them that, Steven had joked, "So all Shawn's baggage must be carry-on."

Jack laughed, but Ashley just looked puzzled.

Morgan snorted. "Carry-on. A pun on carrion, which is what condors eat. Dead animals are called carrion. Jeez, Ashley, what grade are you in?"

"Why don't you go flame yourself," she answered in a fake sweet voice.

Now Shawn greeted them with, "Hi. I guess you're Olivia and Steven Landon. I'm Shawn."

Olivia introduced Jack and Ashley, who shook hands with Shawn, and then Morgan, who kept his hands behind his back.

Getting right to the point, Olivia said, "The most puzzling part of all about this problem with the condors is the lead pellets. The report here says that they're all different sizes. Is that correct?"

Shawn nodded. "We have no clue about where these are coming from. It's pretty weird."

"Could we see the x-rays that show the lead pellets? Do you keep them here?" Olivia asked.

"Yes. In the back. Follow me."

Morgan said nothing, yet Jack had the sense that Morgan was pretty interested in what was happening, and Ashley noticed it, too. "Morgan likes anything to do with death," she whispered.

Jack told her to hush, glancing quickly at Morgan

to see if he'd heard, but his face had closed off in a way that Jack couldn't read.

The six of them crowded into a small room while Shawn held up the first x-ray in front of a light screen. It felt strange to look at the insides of a big bird. When he was seven, Jack had seen an x-ray of his own broken arm, but this x-ray looked like a turkey carcass after the Landons had demolished it on Thanksgiving. Seven lead pellets inside the condor's intestinal tract stood out in bright white in the dark x-ray, like a constellation of stars on a cloudy night. A second x-ray film showed five pellets. "See, the pellets are different sizes," Shawn said, pointing.

"Maybe they got melted down during the condor's digestion," Ashley suggested, "and some just got digested more than others."

Jack gave Ashley an elbow in the ribs for saying something so unscientific, but Shawn answered, "Actually, they do erode when they get digested."

Ashley jabbed Jack with a triumphant return elbow.

"Which is why we try to get the pellets out as soon as possible—sometimes by tube, sometimes by surgery. We move fast so the lead won't get into the bloodstream. But we don't think digestion is the reason for the difference in pellet size. That part's a mystery. We think it's a key to finding the source of the lead, but…." He scratched at his beard. "Like I said, no one has a clue what it all means."

"Could you please explain why the pellet size is so important?" Steven asked.

"Because we think these birds are all being poisoned from the same source—from a single kill. There are three distinct pellet sizes in all of the intestinal tracts. Although it's possible that these pellets all came from one gun, it is also conceivable that the kill was shot at by at least three different guns. So, whatever animal was killed had to be big—big enough for a group of condors to feed on, anyway."

"Except there's a problem with your theory," Morgan broke in. "Nobody shoots big game with a shotgun." When they all looked at him, he said, "I have an online friend named Snipe. I've learned about guns. Anything large is taken out with a rifle."

"*Snipe?*" Ashley mouthed to Jack, but Jack shook his head at her.

"You're absolutely right about that, Morgan," Shawn agreed. "It doesn't make sense that one large animal was killed with a bunch of shotguns and left to rot. Shotguns are normally used for birds—duck hunting, that sort of thing. But a group of condors are not going to feed on a single dead duck, so that's not the answer." He sighed a long sigh as though he'd gone over every possibility.

Ashley's hand darted up with anticipation. "Oh, I have an idea! Couldn't one shell be filled up with those different-size pellets?"

"No way," Morgan answered. "You can't mix pellets together in one shell, or the gun will blow up in your hand." When they all looked at him, he said, "What?"

"Your friend Snipe sure taught you a lot about guns," Ashley stated.

Morgan's eyebrows moved up. "Your point is…?"

"Let's get back to what we know. What's the largest number of pellets any condor has ingested so far?" Olivia asked.

Shawn answered without missing a beat. "Seventeen."

"Seventeen!" Olivia gasped. "That's a *lot* of lead!"

"Right. Unfortunately, we didn't find the pellets until after the bird was dead." Shawn went on to tell them about a condor called 65—none of the condors had names, only numbers.

"When we did the necropsy—"

Morgan murmured to Jack, "That means an autopsy on animals."

"—it turned up 17 lead pellets in 65's intestinal tract. It's a similar story with all the others." Shawn looked grim, then brightened to say, "On a happier note, we've rehabilitated number 87, and if you like, Olivia, you can come see him. He's ready to be released, but we have to keep him penned up until we find the source of the lead. We can't risk another death."

Olivia answered, "All of us would love to see a condor. The kid's have been dying to get a look at one since we got here."

"It's a rare treat," Shawn agreed. "I only hope the magic of these condors will never end—they belong in the Grand Canyon."

They'd have to ride with him, Shawn said, in The Peregrine Fund's big Ford sports utility four-by-four, because the Landons' rental car would never make it up the rugged back road to the release site. The dirt road turned out to be rough, for sure—a bumpy, dusty, rutted washboard that snaked and twisted as it climbed, gaining 2,000 feet in altitude from the base of the cliffs to the top. During the long drive, Shawn told them how every day, the team members stayed out in the field from dawn to dusk, changing their locations as they held up antennas to try to track signals from the condors' radio transmitters.

"Some condors wear their transmitters on their wings," he said. "We bolt them in place."

"Bolt them!" Ashley exclaimed. "You mean you use real bolts? If I were a condor, that would make me really mad."

"Well, maybe you'd like the other method better. Guess how we attach the transmitters when we put them on the tails."

"I don't know. How?"

Shawn grinned at her in the SUV's rear-view mirror. "With dental floss and Super Glue. Real high-tech." That made all of them laugh, even Morgan.

"If you've got transmitters, can't you track where

they're eating the poison meat?" Jack asked suddenly.

"I wish we could. These transmitters are accurate only within a limited range and only if the signal is aimed at the antenna. We're researching a new kind of tracking device that bounces signals off orbiting satellites. This system would tell us not only where a bird is but also give a record of where it has been. Once we're sure the system will work, we'll begin using it to track our condors."

When Shawn finally stopped the vehicle, he told them, "This is as far as we ride. The last quarter mile, we hike."

The hike was easy enough, winding through low-to-the-ground, fresh-smelling juniper and piñon trees. A breeze cooled them as they crossed the wide plateau at the top of the cliffs. "This is where you guys will stay," Shawn told them, pointing to a pen constructed of plywood and wooden 2-by-4s. Green, military-type netting draped across juniper branches camouflaged the pen like a hunting blind. Until they were practically on top of it, Jack hadn't even noticed it.

"You'll be able to get good pictures from here, Steven and Jack. This is where we always put photographers when we're doing a condor release," Shawn explained.

"Where will you be?" Steven asked.

"Olivia and I will go to the release pen. It's about 50 yards from here, close to the edge of the cliff."

"Why can't we go?" Ashley wanted to know.

"Too many of you. It's not that you would scare the condors—it's just that we don't want them getting used to being around groups of people. Then they start landing near tourists at the Grand Canyon, looking for handouts—it's a bad scene. Understand?"

Jack shrugged and nodded. Under his breath, Morgan said, "Bummer."

"We'll see you later," Olivia called back to them, keeping her voice soft so she wouldn't disturb the condor up ahead.

Inside the cover of the green mesh netting, Steven set up his tripod. "Better attach your telephoto lens," he instructed Jack. "And be alert. Seeing a condor is a rare treat, so don't try to conserve film. Just aim and shoot."

"Calling a bird Number 87 is lame," Morgan said. "You know what I'd name a condor if I owned one? Flip. Flip the Bird."

"Ha ha," Ashley said, giving Morgan a withering look. "You are *so* not funny."

Steven, busy with his cameras, told Jack, "Look sharp, now. You don't want to miss this."

Through his telephoto lens, Jack could watch everything happening in the flight pen. Shawn, followed by Olivia, approached Condor 87—the number was clearly visible on the bird's wing. The bird cocked his bald, orange head as though wondering what these humans were up to. Slowly, Shawn reached out; 87

seemed to know him. The condor waited, unmoving. Shawn knelt and put an arm around 87, holding him close in a man-to-bird hug.

"I think Shawn's checking 87's transmitter now," observed Steven, who was watching through his own telephoto lens.

Then, carefully, Shawn stood up, still holding 87, allowing Olivia to examine the bird. Jack could see his mother enjoying the rare opportunity to handle a creature only a heartbeat away from extinction. As Jack snapped a flurry of pictures, the condors' fight somehow became his.

There had to be a way to save them.

CHAPTER FOUR

Jack knocked on the door that connected the room he shared with Morgan to the room occupied by his parents and Ashley. "Mom, can I borrow your laptop computer?" he asked through the door.

"What for?"

"I have to write a paper about the condors. For science class. The teacher told me the only way she'd excuse me from class was if I wrote a paper—

The door opened.

"And I want to put down all the stuff I learned from Shawn today before I forget it," Jack added, lowering his voice, liking the way it sounded when he didn't have to yell. His voice seemed to be getting deeper lately.

"Are you sure?" Olivia asked, throwing a glance toward Morgan, who was sprawled on his twin bed reading one of the Grand Canyon newspapers. Jack knew what his mother really meant: "Are you sure you want my laptop for homework, and not so Morgan can play on it?" She didn't say that out loud, but Jack read her thoughts.

"Homework. Honest."

"All right, then. Don't use the battery—use the adapter and plug it in."

The motel room was small. Its only surface other than the two beds and a dresser top was a small round table, and Morgan had thrown his clothes all over the tabletop. Jack removed them and put them on the dresser, which was already cluttered with Morgan's shoes and backpack.

He sat down to work on his paper. "The Use of Lead Shotgun Pellets Endangers Condors," he wrote for a title, and then he tried to remember that morning—the x-rays showing lead, the drive up the rutted road to the release pen, the thrilling sight of Condor 87, alive and well now.

Morgan stayed silent as Jack grew absorbed in his writing. When Jack finally glanced at the other bed, Morgan had fallen asleep. After Jack turned off the computer, he pulled off his jeans and crawled into bed. It was late—past eleven—and he fell asleep quickly.

When he woke up, dawn had just begun to seep over the trees and through the window. Morgan was sitting at the round table, hunched over the laptop.

"How long have you been awake?" Jack asked.

"Who needs sleep?" Morgan answered. "Want to take a look?"

Without moving his eyes from the screen, Morgan said, "I had to get back into the game. The other gamers thought I'd quit because it was too tough. Crazy! No game ever beat me yet, and Splatterfest II isn't going to be the first."

Splatterfest II. Jack had never heard of it until Morgan mentioned it the day before. He watched wide-eyed. These graphics were as sizzling as Morgan had described, and even more heart-pumping than his hype. Morgan was playing with another online friend named Dragon; even though more than a thousand miles separated them, Morgan played intensely, and Jack began to get drawn into the action as if the fight were taking place in real time and space. Whooping whenever Morgan made a kill, Jack got so involved he almost forgot where he was; their room at Yavapai Lodge practically melted from his consciousness.

It wasn't until he heard his mother's voice that he mentally snapped back into the dim room, with its striped carpet and air that smelled of fresh sheets and disinfectant. Morgan seemed startled as well, nearly knocking the laptop onto the floor.

"Morgan! What are you doing with my laptop?"

"I—I'm showing Jack some totally crackin' graphics," Morgan answered. "I just hooked it up, and here we are. Your man Jack seems to like it."

That was true. Jack had never before seen anything like the dazzling display before him, but he sensed that now was not the time to admit this to his mother.

"What has he been playing?" The question was directed at Jack. Sensing no way out except to lie, which he wasn't about to do, he muttered, "Splatterfest II."

"Splatterfest II." Olivia nodded, her mouth set hard. "Jack, you know how I feel about these kinds of games."

"Yeah, but the thing is Morgan and his friend Dragon were already really far in this one, and Morgan wanted to show me—"

Waving her hand to silence him, she said coldly, "Morgan, would you please unhook my laptop and get it back into my room? Just to be perfectly clear, I don't want you exposing my kids to games like that."

"You afraid of a few pixels, Mrs. Landon?" Even though Morgan's voice stayed calm, it had a challenge to it.

Olivia answered slowly, spacing every word. "I despise the way they turn violence and death into entertainment. I've read that some gamers begin to act out the violence in real life."

"Is that a fact?" Morgan answered, leaning back into his seat and cocking his head. "Death, in and of itself, can be pretty interesting, don't you think, Mrs. Landon? People have always been fascinated by the macabre, and so am I. But that doesn't mean I'm going to kill somebody. At least," he said, smiling slowly, "not yet."

That's when Jack heard the shift in his mother's voice. It became as detached and arid as a dried leaf floating on the wind. "An interesting point of view, Morgan. I'd love to discuss it, but right now I'm on my way to park headquarters. The rest of you get dressed and go to the cafeteria for breakfast. I'll meet you there in an hour. And Jack, I intend to speak to you later."

#

"This cafeteria's like the United Nations," Jack said as he picked up a plastic tray and slid it along the metal rails. "Listen to all those different languages. People must come here from all over the world."

"Yeah. Uh-huh." Morgan eyed a giggling group of Japanese girls ahead of him in the line. "Man, do I wish I could speak Japanese."

"Sure, Morgan," Jack joked. "And I know what you'd talk to them about—Pokémon, Japanimation, and Quake Three."

"I have a few other topics of conversation," he replied, smoothing the wrinkles out of his T-shirt. "Watch and learn."

The girls, who looked as though they were in their mid-teens, seemed to be subtly checking out Morgan and Jack. Olivia, Steven, and Ashley were in a separate breakfast line, one that featured more healthy food. Since Jack had already been through the healthy line, he just followed Morgan as he piled his plate with waffles and pancakes, first smothering the top with whipped butter followed by an oozing layer of syrup. Very quickly the girls dismissed Jack as too young, but one of them smiled at Morgan. "How you doing?" he asked, thrusting out his chin and then raising his hand in a friendly gesture that knocked a glass of orange juice all over his tray.

The Japanese girls were really giggling now, but softly, as though they didn't want to embarrass Morgan even more. "Smooth, Morgan," Jack snickered.

"Yeah, well." Pushing his dark hair from his forehead, he muttered, "Relationships with women are highly overrated."

"As if you would know," Ashley quipped, joining them from behind. Sliding her tray behind Jack's, she grabbed a chocolate milk and placed it next to her cereal bowl, watching with interest as the Japanese girls slid their trays up to the cashier and paid, speaking in halting English. Since there was a group of them, Jack figured it would take a while.

Morgan gave Ashley a withering look. "It just so happens I do know. It may surprise you to find out that I was voted Homecoming King in my high school."

"Sure you were." She rolled her eyes at Jack.

"It's true. Of course, I hacked into the school's computer and rigged the results. But I officially won."

"You went to the dance as Homecoming King?" Jack

asked. He couldn't believe what Morgan was saying.

"No, actually I stayed home and missed all the excitement. Heard about it, though." He took a step closer to the register. "My one regret is that I didn't see Queenie's face when the big moment came. I guess she curled up when my name was read out—she thought she'd actually have to dance with me. When they finally figured I was a no-show, some Neanderthal got crowned as king instead. Yeah," he said, nodding smugly, "that was one of my better hacker stings."

"You *ruined* Homecoming?"

Shrugging, Morgan said, "I added a bit of color to the proceedings."

"No. You broke into a computer and changed the results so the Homecoming Queen got to stand there, all by herself, while you stayed at home and laughed at her. How could you be so mean?" Ashley asked fiercely. The Japanese girls were gone now, but Ashley didn't move and neither did Morgan. "I bet she spent a ton of money on her dress, getting her hair done and makeup, and then you just messed it up!"

"I believe in payback," he said, his voice suddenly low. "She was vicious to me, and she got what she deserved. Those who don't want retribution better stay out of my way."

"So you always have to win, right?"

"Yeah," Morgan replied. "Always."

The two of them stood toe to toe, Ashley's eyes

burning into Morgan's cool ones while the line of customers behind them swelled to four-deep. Why couldn't they get along, even for five minutes? Jack thought wearily. The lady running the cash register waved them forward.

"Come on, guys, you're holding things up." Jack tried to nudge his sister toward the cash register.

"Jack, what he did—"

"I know, but it's over, and it's not worth fighting about, especially not here."

"Why are you always on Morgan's side?"

"I'm not!"

"Yes you are. Don't you see what he's doing?"

"What *am* I doing, Ashley?" Morgan loomed over her, his pale face expressionless. "Why don't you tell me?"

A customer, a small, mousy-looking man with a dingy mustache scurried by, while a woman with skin as dark as coffee murmured, "Excuse me," and pushed around them.

"Just forget it," Ashley said finally. "I'm done." Without another word she shoved her tray toward the register, but at the last minute she turned and said, "I know what you are, Morgan. You can play your game with my dad and Jack, but you don't fool my mom. And you don't fool me."

Smiling slowly, Morgan said, "Then let the games begin."

CHAPTER FIVE

Back stiff as a board, Ashley made her way around the tables to where her parents sat, while Jack paid for his and Morgan's breakfast. As Morgan followed Jack through the clutter of chairs and chatting tourists, both of them held their trays high to avoid knocking anyone on the head.

"You know, your sister is extremely touchy," Morgan told Jack.

"Nah, Ashley's cool."

"Then why do I get the same feeling from her that I did from the kids in Dry Creek, namely that everything I say is wrong. I don't understand the reason my words always land me in a pile knee-deep. Hold on a second." He stopped between two tables, resting his tray on a bony hip. "What she said back there—is it true? Are you on my side?"

Jack thought he knew what Morgan was asking,

but this didn't seem the place to go into it. The cafeteria was crowded and noisy, his food was getting cold, and anyway, how was he supposed to answer a question like that? Even if he'd known how, he didn't want to. "Let's go," was all he said.

Steven and Olivia had settled in next to a group of older women who seemed in good spirits for so early in the morning, laughing and chattering between swigs of coffee. At 8:30 a.m., the cafeteria's noise level kept escalating with the sound of rattling silverware, sputtering coffee urns, ringing cash registers and banging trays. Above the mechanical clatter, tourists of many colors and styles of dress called out to each other in half a dozen different languages.

"We saved you a place," Steven called out, patting the Formica tabletop. After they had settled into their seats, Jack took his yogurt, banana, and scrambled eggs off his plastic tray and placed them symmetrically on the table, banana pointing north, yogurt positioned at ten o'clock next to the plate. Morgan, who hadn't bothered to remove his plate from the tray, was already digging into his stack of pancakes drowned with syrup. For a skinny kid, he sure could put away the pancakes.

Olivia sipped her coffee, then gave him a forced smile. "Morgan, I woke up last night thinking about something you said earlier. It was about the pellets and the shotguns. How do you know so much about this?"

"I told you, my friend, Snipe. He's the one who

introduced me to Splatterfest II," Morgan answered around a mouthful of pancake. "That game is serious eye candy, with the most fluid graphics in the world of CGI. It's been around for a while, but in this new version the texture quality is better, the frame rate has been upped, and the integration between real-time polygons and CGI is awesome. I admit, you could maybe say the designers programmed elements from the entire RPG genre, but it still has plenty of new stuff, too."

Jack hadn't a clue what all that meant, but he didn't want to seem stupid in front of Morgan. "RPG?" he asked hesitantly. "Red, *purple*, green? I thought—uh—aren't images made from RGB? Red, green, blue?"

Morgan stopped chewing to give Jack a pitying look. "RPG means 'role-playing game.'"

"I knew that," Jack said quickly.

Olivia carefully set down her mug. "Back to my shotgun question; did you learn about pellets from this Splatterfest game?"

"Nah. Splatterfest's all high-tech weaponry. I guess I learned the low-tech stuff from following the Predator Hunt. Snipe's into that real big."

"Predator Hunt?"

"You haven't heard of it? I thought you were an animal guru. The hunt is like Splatterfest, only the targets are real critters. Too grim for me, but Snipe's a follower."

Olivia took a breath and released it between her

teeth. "Morgan, I have a favor to ask," she said. "I need you to contact your friend Spike."

"Snipe," Morgan answered.

"Right. Snipe. Could you reach Snipe for me? I'm trying to unravel the pellet mystery, specifically how they're used in shotgun shells, but none of the park people hunt. Would Snipe discuss it, do you think?"

"If I tell him to." Morgan dismissed the question with a wave of his hand. "What would be even better is getting you right on the hunt Web site. Snipe showed it to me. Start there."

"Thank you, Morgan."

"Not a problem. I'd like to point out that no matter what people say, everyone eventually comes to the geeks. We rule."

Back at the motel, it took Morgan only a moment to tap into the Predator Hunt Web site, while Steven, Ashley, Olivia and Jack crowded around to watch.

"Here it is," Morgan announced, triumphant. The blue screen announced, in big, bold letters, ANNUAL VARMINT HUNT. CASH-FOR-CARCASSES CONTEST. KILL A BUNCH OF PREDATORS AND HELP WILDLIFE. FIRST PRIZE $50,000. Beneath these words were pictures of a fox, a coyote, a bobcat, and a mountain lion.

Next to the pictures of the animals was a list of points: 100 for killing a mountain lion; 50 for a bobcat; 25 for a coyote; and 10 for a fox. Printed instructions said hunters were supposed to shoot as many of these creatures as they could within a 24-hour period, then bring the dead animals to a checkpoint, where the bodies could be counted. The hunters' scores would be verified, with prizes awarded to those with the highest scores.

"I can't believe this," Olivia cried, turning bright red with anger. "This is not hunting—it's murder! What kind of friends do you have, Morgan?"

"Take it easy," Steven told her.

"You say Snipe participates in this free-for-all?"

"Yeah. The contest is legal. Any hunter with a license can take part. He's got a license. He says they do it all over the country." Morgan shifted uneasily. He was not enjoying this conversation.

"A license to pile up carcasses for a reward? Hunting laws were created with the idea that when you kill game, you use the meat. This—this is—*body-count* killing. It's slaughter, not hunting," Olivia declared. "Unethical in the extreme."

"Snipe sees it differently. And I don't want you talking to him if you're going to go ballistic about the hunt," Morgan insisted.

"That's the point. This isn't a hunt—" Olivia sputtered to a stop and then began again, "Take a look at the pictures on this screen." She tapped her index finger on each face as she spoke. "A fox. A bobcat. A mountain lion, for heaven's sake. Who ever made the decision that these were varmints? The word 'varmints' is supposed to mean 'useless predators.'"

"This is so gross," Ashley said, glaring at Morgan.

"Hey everybody, let's take it down a notch," Steven broke in. "Morgan isn't the one participating in the hunt. He's trying to help us get information. We'll get to Snipe's Web site and see what we can learn about the guns. Morgan, do you have his Web address?"

"Yeah, sure. It'll just take a second to bring it up, Morgan said, looking relieved to have an excuse to get away from the Predator Hunt page. After he punched in a string of numbers and letters, a jagged mountain peak appeared, followed by an animated hunter with a spitting automatic gun. It hit a target that blew apart into a thousand blood-red pieces.

"Snipe's always been into cool graphics," Morgan said sheepishly. "I have to warn you, he talks a lot about the government and conspiracies, but that's just his politics. He's good at gaming."

"Yes, he seems to have a lot of opinions about a lot of things," Steven agreed, inspecting the screen.

"When are you going to write your question about the pellets?" Jack asked, pressing to get a better look. Beneath bold headlines Snipe had written blocks of text, but Jack couldn't get close enough to read it. Steven's and Olivia's heads were in the way.

"This is quite a Web site," Steven murmured. "He talks about the predator hunt here, and there's a list of preferred guns…then all kinds of…." Steven's voice trailed off. Blue backlight turned his skin gray as he scrolled through graphics and other blocks of text, moving from one line to the next.

"Do you see that?" Olivia's face suddenly hardened. She looked at Steven, whose own jaw had set. "Are you reading what I'm reading?"

Nodding tersely, Steven answered, "I see it."

"See what?" Jack asked, trying to get a look. Whatever it was, his parents hid it as they moved closer together. Olivia looked as though an ice storm was raging behind her eyes, Morgan kept rubbing his chin with the tips of his fingers, and Ashley had turned deathly quiet.

"Jack, I'd like you and Ashley to go into the other room," Olivia ordered. "Right now. Morgan, stay here."

"What'd I do?"

"I think you know," Steven answered.

"Can't I stay and—" Jack began, but when he saw his mother's face, his voice dried up in his throat. "Come on, Ashley," he said quickly, retreating through the door.

The moment the door shut a flood of muffled words erupted from the other side. Jack couldn't understand them, but he didn't have to. His mother was angrier than she had ever been with Morgan, that much was certain. His father, who had usually been so quick to defend, now accused him, his deep voice rising and falling between Olivia's staccato outbursts.

"What the heck is going on?" Jack whispered to

Ashley, not so much to keep from being overheard but to keep from missing any possible bit of conversation he might decipher from the next room.

"I don't know for sure. I just—I saw my name."

Jack felt his heart pump faster. "Where?"

"On that Web site. I'm pretty sure that Snipe guy wrote something bad about me. It was under a head-line that said, 'Government Injustice.'"

"That can't be right—Snipe doesn't even know you."

"Morgan does. I think he sent one of those flame things to Snipe, and Snipe posted it."

"Morgan wouldn't do that! When could he have—no way, Ashley!" Jack shook his head hard, more for himself than for his sister. He pressed his ear against the door, but the sound was still too muffled for him to make out individual words. Ashley stomped over to him, her hands on her hips and her head high.

"Of *course* Morgan would never dream of doing the same thing to me that he did to everyone in Dry Creek! You *always* think the best of him."

"No, you always think the worst of him! Look, he's weird, but he wouldn't do that to you."

"Wanna bet? I'll crack open the door, and then we'll find out if I'm right."

"You mean eavesdrop?"

"Duh! Don't you want to know the real story and not some lie Morgan tells you? You do what you want. I'm listening."

With that, Ashley put her hand on the knob and turned it so slowly it was barely perceptible. She opened the door cautiously, creating a space less than an inch wide. It made all the difference, like turning up the volume on the television. Jack could suddenly understand every word spoken in the next room.

"...about her. Snotty? Arrogant?"

"Hey, I was letting off steam. I didn't know he'd post it. Snipe's mad about the way the government broke in and took me away from my home. He's using what happened to me as an example."

"When did you write the e-mail?" This from Steven.

"While you were at the Grand Canyon, that first morning." Morgan's voice sounded tight as he continued, "But I wouldn't write the same stuff now. Try to understand, my freedom was taken away, and I was mouthing off to a friend. It doesn't *mean* anything."

Inside, Jack groaned. So it was true. Morgan had flamed Ashley. How dumb could he be?

Olivia's voice was sharp. "I'm afraid it means a great deal to me."

"But I swear, I didn't know Snipe would post it. Blame him, not me."

"You're always the victim," Olivia snapped. "The thing is, Morgan, I can take the harsh words you wrote about me. You think I'm a brainless, government pawn whose joy is suppressing your freedom? Fine. I'm an adult. I can take your nastiness. But I can't—no, I *won't* allow you to trash my daughter. It's obvious to me that bringing you here was a mistake."

"Olivia!"

"I mean it, Steven. I want to call Ms. Lopez and see if other arrangements can be made."

"You can't do that! I'll be sent to juvenile detention," Morgan cried. "Mr. Landon—"

"You should have thought of the consequences before you wrote that e-mail," Olivia insisted.

"I don't want to go!"

Olivia's voice was equally forceful. "This isn't about what you want. Look, I have a CNN interview to do, and then Steven and I will decide on the next step. For now, I don't want Ashley to know what was said on that Web site. Is that clear?"

"I'm supposed to obey you when you want to ditch me?"

"OK, OK, let's all calm down here," Steven broke in. "Morgan, this is an important interview for Olivia. We're all going to go and support her. Behave yourself, and then we'll see what's next."

Jack carefully pulled the door shut and tried to swallow the knot that had tightened his throat. His sister was hurt, his mother was angry, Morgan was being sent away, and the condors were still dying. How could this trip get any worse?

CHAPTER SIX

Morgan hunched so low in the backseat of the car that his knees almost touched his chin. Outside, the park slid by, its small, snug buildings overrun by people scurrying about like ants. Inside the car, no one spoke—silence crept around them like a thick, choking cloud. Olivia checked the map and gave instructions on how to get to Mather Point; Steven answered briefly, then lapsed once again into the silence. Jack suspected that they were quiet because they were replaying the conversation that had taken place moments before about the Web site and the fact that Morgan might have to leave. Although Ashley wasn't letting on that she'd listened in, Jack could tell how angry she was. She dug her fingernails into her palm until little half-moon marks made a pattern on her skin.

"Look, we all should talk. Morgan, I've been thinking," Olivia began, turning in her seat. She hesitated then gave a forced smile. "On reflection I can see the condor deaths have really put a strain on me, so, well, perhaps I overreacted back in the hotel room."

"What did Morgan do?" Ashley asked, pretending she hadn't heard the whole conversation.

"I'll tell you about it later, sweetheart. For now, I think I need to apologize to Morgan for some things I said." Reaching out her hand, she said, "I'd like to bury the hatchet."

Morgan didn't answer. He planted his elbows on his knees, lacing his fingers around the back of his neck.

"Did you hear what I said?"

"Yeah, you said you want to bury the hatchet. Where—in my back?"

"Morgan!" Steven exploded.

Olivia sighed and faced front again. "It's OK," she told Steven. "I tried. Look, I want to get my head focused on this interview. Ashley, is my hair OK?" she asked, deliberately changing the subject. "It feels like it's going wild."

"You look great, Mom," Ashley assured her. With the tips of her fingers, she smoothed the back of her mother's hair. "Really. Hey, look at the crowd!"

A lot of tourists had already gathered in the parking lot, excited about the two cameramen with their CNN logos. As Olivia got out of the car, a woman in a trench coat took her arm, saying, "Would you come over this way, Dr. Landon? We need to test the mike."

Olivia tossed a smile in a backward glance to her family, and then took off toward the CNN news truck.

"Mom's going to be a celebrity," Ashley exclaimed. "If she gets famous, will she still cook for us?"

"Well, if she doesn't, I will," Steven answered, tugging a lock of Ashley's dark hair to tease her. Steven wore the usual warm, fond expression that he saved for Ashley. Maybe it was because she was like a smaller version of Olivia, with dark, curly hair, big, dark eyes, and a petite build. To Jack, Steven showed his affection in a different way, ruffling his hair, giving him pretend punches to the biceps, grabbing him playfully around the back of the neck to pull him close for a quick, manly hug. Just as Ashley looked like their mother, Jack looked like their dad: almost a clone, in fact—tall and thin, blue-eyed, with stick-straight blond hair.

"Come on, we want to find a good spot where we can see and hear everything," Steven said. "I wonder if this will be telecast live? Maybe I ought to get the cell phone and call your grandparents."

As Steven hurried back to the car for the cell phone, Morgan asked Jack, "How does your dad feel when people make so much fuss over your mother?"

"What do you mean? He feels fine about it. Why wouldn't he?"

Morgan shrugged. "I dunno. I was just thinking about my own parents. In my house, my dad's the total boss. Like, if our family had taken in a foster kid, there'd be no way my dad would let my mom throw the kid out. But I guess your mom's the one who rules the Landon family, right? What she says goes."

"My mom is not going to throw you out, Morgan. Not if you act decent, anyway. Why were you so obnoxious when she was trying to talk to you in the car?"

"I have a long cool-down period when I'm mad. Did you know your mom said she wanted me to leave?"

"No. Well—yeah," Jack admitted.

Again, Morgan raised his eyebrows and shrugged. "So I get sent back like defective software. Only it's not going to happen. I'm not going to just sit back and get sent to detention."

What's that supposed to mean? Jack wondered. He was about to ask when Ashley raised her finger to her lips. *Shhh,* they're putting Mom on camera now."

With his aspiring-photographer's eye, Jack glanced at the cliffs to check the scene where his mother was going to stand, with her back to the canyon, facing the cameras. It seemed a perfect background—red-orange vertical fractures and pinnacles in the Kaibab limestone along the rim, green trees whose roots would eventually crumble part of the rocks, ravens winging overhead. The vivid blue sky framed Olivia's dark hair as it ruffled in the breeze; the same breeze lifted the rust-colored silk scarf she'd slung around her neck. Wearing a black leather belted jacket over stonewashed jeans, she seemed almost too young to have a teenage son.

Jack felt a swelling of pride. Not only had the park turned to his mother for answers on the condor mystery, but the whole nation was listening to what she had to say.

"Three, two, one," a cameraman said, counting down with his fingers before pointing at Olivia. As the cameramen started to roll their film, the trench-coat lady spoke into the microphone. "This is Claudia Franklin, here on the rim of the magnificent Grand Canyon. Next to me is Dr. Olivia Landon, wildlife veterinarian and specialist in endangered species. Dr. Landon, you've been telling me about a serious problem with the condors. Could you give us more details about this lead poisoning that threatens them?"

Looking relaxed, with her hands in her pockets, Olivia answered, "I'd be happy to, Claudia. There was a time when these big, graceful birds soared all over the Southwest. Then in the 1800s settlers moved West, and the condors suffered. By the 1980s, there were fewer than 30 California condors in the world."

"What caused the decline?" Claudia asked.

"Oh, shootings, electrocution from power lines, poisoning, attacks by golden eagles. Also, condors don't reproduce very fast. Mature females may lay only one egg every two years. The number of captive birds, the ones in zoos, became fairly stable, but condors in the wild began to become more and more scarce. In 1987, the last one was removed from the wild and placed in captivity."

Not waiting for Claudia to ask another question, Olivia continued, "Then the captive-breeding program in zoos began to produce enough condors that scientists decided to reintroduce some of them into the wild—in California and north of here at the Vermilion Cliffs. Those condors did well, until—"

"What happened?" Claudia asked, right on cue.

"They began to sicken and die. From lead poisoning. Condors feed on carrion—dead animals. If condors eat a carcass shot with lead pellets and they ingest the lead, it can kill them. *Has* killed at least three of them in the past few months, and maybe more. What we don't understand is the source of all this lead. That's why I'm here."

Claudia shook her head in concern. "Can anything be done to stop the deaths?"

"Yes!" Olivia spoke so vehemently that Jack jumped, and a soft murmur went through the crowd of people gathered in a semicircle to watch the interview. "First, let me say, Claudia, that the team of scientists and park rangers trying to save these birds are the most dedicated people I've ever known. They work every day—and I mean every day, no time off—to help the condors. After the five deaths, they recaptured almost all of the wild condors in this area and have kept them caged for the birds' safety. That means they have to remain locked away until the source of the contamination is located. The last bird, an adolescent they call

Number 72, has just been spotted in the area of Grandeur Point, which is where I'll be for the rest of the day. When that condor is caught, visitors will once again be deprived of experiencing these magnificent birds."

"What can be done?" Claudia prompted.

"The most obvious solution is for hunters to stop using shotgun shells that contain lead pellets. Other types of shells are available that won't hurt the condors. Oh, I know it would cost a little more, but responsible hunters are already changing to non-lead ammunition."

"Do you believe all the hunters will comply?"

Olivia shook her head no. "We already know some will not do this voluntarily. And so, I want to propose a more drastic solution."

Half watching the cameramen, Jack got the impression that they now zoomed in for a close-up. Maybe Claudia had given them some kind of signal. "And what is your plan, Dr. Landon?"

"I propose that a law be passed," Olivia said, pausing for effect, "that would ban all lead-pellet shells within 200 miles of the boundaries of Grand Canyon National Park. Anyone using lead shot would be subject to a hefty fine and possible jail time."

Claudia turned to look directly into the cameras. "That sounds like a drastic proposal. Won't there be a lot of opposition?"

"Not from responsible hunters."

"What about the perception among certain hunters

that the government is already assuming the role of "Big Brother" in regulating the use of their guns? Many gun owners complain that they are being unfairly targeted by environmentalists. What is your response to them?"

"Well, to put it simply, my concern is for the condors. Condors need protection, even it that means stepping on a few hunters' toes."

"But is passing a new law the right approach?"

"It's the only option I can see. Legal action will be necessary because people don't always do the right thing of their own volition. Regulations have to be made and then enforced in order to protect animals."

"Can you give me an example?" Claudia prompted.

Olivia paused for just a moment before saying, "Yes, an example of this would be the Cash-for-Carcasses hunts, something I just learned about today. Most hunters would never even think about participating in this wholesale slaughter, but a minority are blasting away at mountain lions, foxes, and certain predators for cash prizes. At this time, this environmentally disastrous kind of hunting is legal. Once again, legislation needs to be passed to protect the animals who can't protect themselves, and I'm committed to doing whatever it takes to stop these abuses."

"Thank you, Dr. Landon." Again, speaking to the cameras, Claudia said, "You've just heard Dr. Olivia Landon, specialist in threatened and endangered species, telling us how she hopes to ban lead shot in order to protect the condors, and also put an end to Cash-for-Carcasses hunts. This is Claudia Franklin, CNN News Hour, reporting from Grand Canyon National Park."

It was over. Applause broke out in the crowd surrounding the scene of the interview, and as Olivia walked toward her family, her face flushed with excitement, people rushed forward to shake her hand and pat her on the back. Many of the people were park rangers, wearing their uniforms of light gray shirts and dark green pants.

"That was terrific, Olivia," a red-haired ranger named Pam told her, and a park biologist with a name tag that said "Elaine" enthused, "I'm so glad you brought that up about the Cash-for-Carcasses hunt. Only, I think I would have been a lot nastier about it than you were. Of course, if I'd said what I really think, they'd have bleeped me off the air."

All the Landons plus Morgan and the CNN team were invited back to park headquarters for something like a victory celebration. They crowded into the park superintendent's office and adjoining meeting room, talking excitedly about Olivia's interview.

"You must be Olivia's daughter," a ranger was saying to Ashley. "You sure look like her. I bet you were real proud of your mother today. And are these your brothers?" he asked, pointing to Jack and Morgan.

"That one is. But the one with the facial fuzz is not

my brother," Ashley answered firmly. "Morgan is the one who showed my mom the Cash-for-Carcasses hunt on the Internet. His friend Snipe goes out and kills animals for prize money, which Morgan thinks is OK."

"Really?" the ranger said disapprovingly.

Suddenly self-conscious, Morgan fingered his attempt at a goatee. When the ranger turned his focus on Jack and Ashley, asking them questions about school and the wildlife around Jackson Hole, Morgan turned and walked away, disappearing into one of the halls. Jack listened as his footsteps echoed down the corridor like soft drumbeats, until no sound but the ranger's rhythmic voice remained.

When the ranger finally left, Jack turned to his sister and demanded, "What you said about Morgan was rude. Why do you have to diss him every chance you get?"

"Why do you care?" she answered. "I thought the ranger should know who Morgan really is. Besides, if you want to talk about rude, Morgan said some bad things about me that got posted on Snipe's Web site. Why aren't you mad about that?"

Jack didn't have a reply, because he wasn't clear about it in his own mind. What Morgan had done was wrong—no one could argue that. But the more Jack got to know Morgan, the more he began to feel that beneath that prickly outside, beyond the smart mouth, a half-decent kid might be lurking somewhere. If Jack's mom sent Morgan away, he might never know who Morgan really was, and the idea bothered him. And yet, what if he discovered that Morgan was even worse than Ashley imagined? When a rock is turned over, ugly things can crawl out.

"Look, Jack," Ashley said, putting her hands on her hips, "I don't want to fight with you. Let's call a truce. I saw some cool stuff in the bookstore gift shop. Want to come with me?"

"No, you go ahead. I'll catch up later."

"You're looking for Morgan, aren't you?"

"Well, yeah. He's disappeared. I just want to know where he's—" But Ashley didn't wait for him to finish.

"Fine, whatever!" she snapped, marching in the direction of the gift shop.

Jack drifted over to where his father was deep in conversation with one of the CNN cameramen, hoping to ask if he'd seen Morgan but afraid to interrupt. He tried to listen to what they were saying, but it was too technical for him, so he wandered around looking for Morgan on his own. Twice he walked up and down the halls, peering through office doors that were lighted but empty before finally stumbling across Morgan coming out of the men's room.

"Hey, where've you been?"

"You checking up on me?" Morgan demanded.

"No. I just wanted to talk."

Eyeing him warily, Morgan asked, "About what?"

"About…I don't know. Nothing, I guess."

"Good!" Morgan broke into the beginnings of a smile. "I've had enough moralizing to last me awhile. I mean, your mom was out of control back there. I hope Snipe doesn't see that report—he would freak if he thought the hunt was going to get banned."

"She's pretty intense when it comes to animals. But everyone in my family is. *I* think that hunt is gross."

"Except no one mentioned that Cash-for-Carcasses shoots mostly coyotes, which reproduce even faster when they're killed off."

"If they're dead, they can't have babies."

"Really?" Morgan asked sarcastically. "I'm talking about when they're thinned out they're fewer of them competing for food, so the survivors' litters get bigger, which means there's no way hunters can ever wipe them out." Nodding with satisfaction, he added, "Snipe told me."

"So? That's still no excuse to use animals for target practice."

Beneath lowered lids, Morgan stared down at Jack. "Everything dies. It's only a matter of when."

"That's the same as saying one human can kill another human because 'they all die anyway.'" Jack could feel the color rising in his cheeks, until he saw the amused grin bending the corners of Morgan's mouth.

"Point taken," Morgan said, giving a slight bow. "But before we leave this subject, I'd like you to consider that if your mom and all her tree-hugging friends are right, then people are just animals on the food chain, which means we shouldn't be held accountable for acting like them since that's all we are. Animals kill each other all the time, right? So we as humans should be entitled to the same privilege. You lose the argument."

"I can*not* follow your logic. You're so weird," Jack answered, shaking his head.

"You just noticed? How unobservant. I'm hungry."

"Me, too. Let's find Ashley and see if we can get my dad to buy us some pizza."

"Deal," Morgan said. "You know, Jack, you're all right. Most people can't take me, but you hang in."

"I guess that makes *me* weird."

"Most definitely," Morgan nodded. "You might even be a geek. That's the next level past weird."

"Please, you're scaring me."

When they begged for pizza, Steven gave in almost immediately. "Let's head for the cafeteria. I could go for a bit of high-carbo, high-fat myself."

In the cafeteria, Olivia began to relax. She talked a bit to Morgan, and this time he answered without a hint of sarcasm. Jack could tell his mother was pleased. Even Ashley seemed to be warming up, especially when Morgan accidentally dropped a slice of pizza down the front of his shirt, leaving a tomato-red smear.

"You certainly have trouble with your food," she snickered. "Orange juice, pizza—maybe you need a bib."

Morgan took the teasing good-naturedly, without even a word of verbal retaliation.

After pizza, back at the Yavapai Lodge, Steven invited the two boys into the room he shared with Olivia and Ashley, saying, "Come on in—Olivia's just going online to check her e-mail. Then we'll head over to Grandeur Point and try to spot the condor."

They waited, Ashley sitting on the cot that had been brought into the room for her, Jack looking at a Grand Canyon map to see where they'd been, Olivia calling up her e-mail on the laptop.

"Oh my! Steven, come look at this," Olivia gasped.

In an instant both Steven and Morgan were behind her. Morgan, peering over Olivia's shoulder, bit his lip and squeezed his eyes shut tightly as Jack and Ashley crowded around. On the pale green, high-resolution computer screen, the message stood out in large, bold, capital letters:

DR LANDON
YOU THINK VARMITS DESERV TO LIVE.
YOUR WRONG. DEAD WRONG. VARMITS
DESERV TO DIE. AND SO DO YOU.

CHAPTER SEVEN

Olivia stared at the screen, her eyes seemingly transfixed by the words. "Well," she said at last, "I guess
someone out there objects to my idea about banning
the varmint hunt."

"Who wrote that?" Steven asked hotly. "Is there a
return address? No, I suppose a coward who would
e-mail something like that would prefer to hide. Just a
gutless thug who won't even sign his name."

Peering more closely at the screen, Olivia said,
"You're right—there's no return address. I never knew
a message could be sent with no return address. How
is that even possible?"

"Actually, it's fairly easy to send an e-mail anony-
mously," Morgan said quietly.

"Yes. I'm sure you would know," Olivia answered.
The comment wasn't meant to sting, but Jack could tell
it hurt Morgan. Color flushed his cheeks and spread all

the way to the tips of his ears, like a creeping burn. A part of Jack felt bad, but knowing that Morgan had set up a nasty Web page of his own and had used his knowledge of the Internet to post his message of scorn—well, better than anyone, Morgan knew how to hit and run. Olivia kept her eyes on the screen. She seemed strangely calm as she read and reread the message. "On the bright side, whoever sent it isn't too awfully sharp. He can't spell."

"Don't take this lightly, Olivia," Steven told her. "This is a threat. This maniac says 'varmits—meaning varmints—deserve to die and *so do you*.' That sounds dangerous. The best thing we can do is call the police."

"That won't do any good—" Morgan began, but Steven cut him off.

"We'll let them decide how to handle it," he snapped. "I'm not going to just sit here and let some wacko threaten my wife! At least the police can properly advise us." He made a move toward the phone, but stopped abruptly when he realized that the phone wouldn't work because the computer was still connected to the phone line.

By then Olivia was at his side, taking his hands in hers. Steven was as fair as Olivia was dark, and her tanned hands looked small, almost childlike in his. "No, Steven, let me do it. I should be the one to call."

"Mom, is someone going to hurt you?" Ashley asked, her voice barely above a whisper.

"Of course not." She flashed Ashley a smile that didn't fool Jack for a second.

"None of you get it—this is just some guy flaming Olivia," Morgan stated matter-of-factly. "People on the Net do it all the time. It doesn't necessarily mean anything. Like I told you, the Internet is a different world, run with different rules." He waved his hand dismissively and said, "Forget the police. They'll never be able to trace a good hacker."

"How do you know?" Ashley demanded, turning on Morgan with an indignation that might have had more to do with fear than anger.

Morgan clenched his fists. "All I'm saying is the police can't help!"

"Did your friend Snipe write it?"

"Snipe wouldn't write garbage like that. And I wouldn't protect him if he did. All I'm telling you is that whoever sent this didn't break the law!"

"*You* sent it, didn't you?" Ashley looked startled, as though the idea itself surprised her, even though it had come from her own lips. "You were mad at my mom because she was going to send you back to Dry Creek!"

"Ashley, how did you know about that?" Olivia gasped.

"I—I was listening in when you guys were talking. I know about what he said about me on Snipe's Web page. Sort of. And now he's going after you!"

Steven took a step toward his daughter. "That's

enough! Morgan didn't have access to your mother's laptop. It's impossible."

"But Dad, he disappeared when we were back at headquarters. Jack went looking for him. He could have gone into an office and e-mailed it from there."

"That is so stupid I'm not even going to answer," Morgan retorted. His eyes had changed from blue to the color of steel, cold and distant. He crossed his arms tightly over his chest.

Jack couldn't stand it another minute. How could his own sister accuse Morgan that way! Sure, Morgan was hard to take, stubborn and smart and arrogant. But Jack knew him better now. The accusation was one hundred percent impossible. "Stop it, Ashley. Morgan wouldn't threaten Mom, and you know it!"

For a second, Ashley looked uncertain. "Look at what he did in Dry Creek," she said defensively. "Think about how he trashed Mom and me—"

"I didn't know Snipe was going to post that and those people in Dry Creek were never my friends—" Morgan shouted at the same time Jack cried, "Oh, come *on*—that's not *anything* like the same thing—"

Suddenly Steven was in the middle of them, thrusting out his hands as though he were a traffic cop. "Hold it! Time out!" he shouted. "This has gone far enough! Everyone stop talking—*now!*"

The room became still, as if the volume button had been switched to mute. Steven looked each one of them full in the face. "All right. That's better. Now listen to me, all of you. We have a problem, and we have to deal with it logically. No more shouting, no more turning on one another—we have to calm down and think this whole thing through carefully. Do you understand what I'm saying?"

Jack and Ashley nodded. Morgan stood, sullen, his eyes locked on the floor.

"Ashley, why don't you and your brother go into the other room for a minute, and see what you can find on TV," Olivia said, putting her arms around Ashley's shoulders and guiding her to the connecting door. "I think your father and I need to talk to Morgan."

"Why do I always have to leave? It's not fair!"

"And why do I always have to stay?" Morgan practically shouted. "You're not taking what she said seriously, are you?"

When Olivia didn't answer, Jack watched the blood drain from Morgan's face. "But I didn't do anything. Great. Perfect. You think I'm guilty, just like that!" Snapping his fingers, he glared at Olivia. "Jack, you don't think I wrote that message, right?"

The question caught him off guard, but before he could think it through he blurted, "No way."

"See—Jack believes me!"

"Son, go into the other room with Ashley. And shut the door, please. Come here, Morgan, and sit down." Olivia's voice was surprisingly cool as she dropped onto the bed and tapped the mattress beside her. Jack would have liked to hear more, but his father nudged him through the door, then shut it, cutting him off. He heard the lock slide in place with a loud click.

For the second time in as many days Jack and Ashley had been shoved into another room while the action went on without them. Why couldn't he be a part of the conversation? Morgan was his friend. Pressing his ear against the rough wood, Jack strained to hear. He could make out voices rising and falling, Morgan's words coming in a rush while his mother's and father's replies sounded muffled. What little Jack could hear was suddenly drowned out by the sound of the television. Ashley was sprawled on the bed, the remote in her hand, flipping through channels as though shuffling cards in a deck. Jack stared at her, anger welling in his throat. He suddenly felt as though he barely knew his own sister.

"Way to go, Ashley," he hissed. "Way to get Morgan in trouble. There's no way he wrote that message, and you know it!"

"Maybe. Maybe not." She punched the button on the remote again and again, ignoring him. "He wrote those awful things on his own Web site."

"So?"

"He changed the votes and messed up the Homecoming dance. When he's mad, he uses a computer. He's been mad at Mom. He wrote bad things about her."

"But he wouldn't say Mom deserved to *die!*"

"Why not? She was going to send him away, remember? But you don't care about the facts, because you two are best friends now. Just you and Morgan. Best friends with the guy who dissed me. But you don't care about that, either."

So that was it, Jack thought, suddenly understanding. How could he have missed the fact that Ashley had been hurt by what Morgan wrote about her? What were the words his mother had read from Snipe's Web page? Jack searched his memory. Snotty. Arrogant. Those statements weren't even close to describing his sister, yet they had been etched on a screen for any and all to see. Still…Morgan had been chewed up and spit out because of how different he was. It made sense that he would fight back in the electronic universe, punching fingers into a keyboard as if they were fists. Morgan walked his own line, but he wouldn't menace Jack's mother.

Jack sighed and dropped onto the bed directly across from Ashley. She didn't look at him, but kept speeding through the channels, never pausing long enough to even guess what the program was about.

"Look, Ashley," Jack began, "Morgan is weird, no question. Maybe I should have punched him when I found out he wrote about you. Hey, maybe I'll still do it, if that'd make you feel better. But this thing with the threat is different. This is real. If Mom and Dad believe he wrote that, he'll be out of here tonight. Maybe not just to detention—maybe to jail!"

Ashley shrugged. The different channels flashed across the screen. Her indifference made him angry all over again. *"He didn't do it,"* Jack cried.

"What if you're wrong?" She threw down the remote and stared at Jack. "You still don't get it, do you? It's like your brain has been taken over by that geek. Guys like Morgan have blown up schools—"

"Wait a minute—where did *that* come from?"

"—but you think he's perfect because he can do a couple of cheap computer tricks. Mom doesn't trust him. *I* think he's dangerous. But *you* don't care what *I* think! You only care about Morgan. *That's* what I'm mad about."

Jack was just about to light into her about the geek comment when the door swung open and their father stood there, looking solemn.

"OK, listen up, we've got a plan," he told them briskly. "Your mother thinks that we need to get a bit of nature to calm us all down. She's going to take you three kids to the rim to watch for the condor. I'll go to park headquarters and at least alert them to what has happened. Then we'll try to put this whole thing behind us and go on. Agreed?"

"Sure," Jack told him, feeling relieved. Getting out of the room seemed like the perfect move. "I'll bring my camera."

"The *three* of us?" Ashley asked in disbelief. "We're

taking Morgan? Why am I the only one who sees what's happening here?" she asked, throwing herself back onto the bed.

"Sweetheart, this trip has been a strain on us all. Things have been said on every side that shouldn't have been said. But after discussing it with Morgan, your mother and I feel—"

"Fine," Ashley said abruptly. She turned off the television and stood up. Her hands were clenched in the pockets of her jeans, but her father didn't notice.

His voice dropped low as he went on, "Look, I know it's been a rough ride for you, Ashley. Morgan has behaved badly towards you, and I'm sorry you even know about it. Your mother and I understand that you were trying to help, but...the bottom line is that neither one of us believes Morgan had anything to do with that message.

"Told you!" Jack said triumphantly.

Steven shot him a look, and anything else Jack was going to say died in his throat.

"I understand why you suspected him. For a bad couple of moments I didn't know what to think myself. But it makes no sense that he would write a message like that. What good would it do?"

Ashley's face contorted. "Couldn't he be trying to scare Mom?"

"Not likely. As Morgan pointed out, he operates under his own code of ethics. Everything he's ever done, right or wrong, has been up front. He attacks his enemies head on."

"That's true, Ashley," Jack agreed.

Steven continued, "Ever since he's been with us, we've jumped on that kid pretty hard. We're supposed to be helping him. Just try to get along, OK? All of you."

Ashley nodded, but her face was like stone.

"The main focus now is to alert the police to that message so we can track down the real culprit. I'm going now," Steven announced. "I'll meet you at the rim in about an hour."

#

Not talking much, they'd started out from Yavapai Lodge, walked past park headquarters, then connected with the Rim Trail, which would take them to the observation station at Yavapai Point. Grand Canyon's rim had warmed with the late-afternoon sun. Jack pulled off his sweatshirt and tied the sleeves around his middle, while Ashley bolted ahead up the paved trail, anxious, it seemed, to get away from the rest of them.

Morgan hung back, his arms swinging loosely at his sides. Since Morgan's sunglasses concealed his eyes, it was hard for Jack to guess what he was thinking. The silence of their half-hour walk had been broken only when Olivia asked questions to try to draw them out. When no one would answer, she'd given up, trusting, she'd said, in the rejuvenating powers of the canyon.

Now, from the trail, Jack realized how right his mother was to bring them here. A wind blew up from the west, tousling his hair and making the pine trees shiver in the sun. Less than 30 feet away, deer munched lazily on wild grass, oblivious to the knots of visitors bustling by. Morgan stopped to watch, while the rest of them walked on. Jack drank in the sweet smell of air tinged with pine and felt himself relaxing. No problem seemed very big next to the Grand Canyon.

"Do you want me to go after Ashley?" Jack asked his mother, his eyes following his sister's retreating figure.

"No, it's OK, let her go, she probably won't walk any farther than the observation building," Olivia answered. She sighed loudly. "I have no clue what's going on with her. After that nasty stuff on Snipe's Web page, I guess I can understand why she's upset with Morgan. I've had a lot of problems with him myself. But it doesn't make any sense that Morgan would break into an office at headquarters, compose a bizarre message, and then pretend not to know anything about it. Still, the idea that it's Morgan has really taken hold of her. Any clues about what's going on with your sister?"

"I—don't know," Jack lied. He didn't want to tell his mother what he suspected. The whole thing had started on the airplane ride, when the lines between Ashley and Morgan had been firmly drawn. Now that Jack was close to the magic of this place, a sense of perspective washed over him—no matter what, Ashley was his sister. He needed to remember that. He shouldn't let her feel as if she didn't matter, or that he'd choose Morgan over her, or that her hurt feelings were stupid.

"Well, I'd better go and try to talk to her," Olivia murmured. "You boys go on to Grandeur Point, if you like, and I'll meet you there."

"No, that's OK," Jack answered quickly. "Let *me* go to Ashley." It would be better to try to fix this himself.

His mother gave him a quizzical look. "You're sure?"

"Yeah. I'm sure."

"All right. I'll call Morgan to catch up to me now, and we'll meet you at Grandeur Point. Don't take too long, though. Keep an eye out for the condor. The last adolescent is supposed to be flying around this area. They're tracking him by radio signal in case he lands, and then they'll try to bring him in. That would really be something to see."

Jack shaded his eyes to look up, but he saw only a sky that was postcard blue and empty, so he continued along the trail.

It didn't take him very long to find Ashley. Dejected, his sister sat on an outlook bench, elbows on knees, her head resting in her hands. Dark hair spilled forward like a veil, cutting her off from the view that captured every other person along the rim. Wordlessly, Jack sat beside her.

After a few minutes he said, "Hi."

"Hi," Ashley answered.

"What are you doing?"

"Sitting here. Where's Morgan?"

"Down with Mom at Grandeur Point. I said we'd meet them there."

"Don't you want to be with him?"

"No."

Ashley raised her head and pushed back her hair. "How come?"

"I don't know. I guess I wanted to talk with you alone. Without fighting."

Ashley didn't answer.

"Look," Jack rushed on, "Some of the things you said about Morgan are true. He's done bad stuff. But I think if you'd give him a chance, you could get past that junk, the way I did."

"So, I take it you're here to tell me to be nice to Morgan. Figures."

"No, that's only part of it. I guess…maybe I've been…." Jack stopped, searching for the right word. Why was talking about this so hard?

"Ignoring me?" Ashley finished for him. "Taking his side? Making me feel like dirt?"

"Yeah. Maybe a little."

"The thing that gets me is that you're blowing me off for Morgan. I mean, he's sick."

"No he's not! OK, Morgan is weird, but he's not the kind of person who would go after Mom. I just don't want you to blame him—you know—because you're mad at me. Oh, man," Jack said, dropping his head into his hands. "I hate stuff like this."

"Like what? Apologizing?"

"Yeah. Like apologizing."

Ashley looked out over the rim, her eyes avoiding Jack's face. "It's not just you. Part of it is about you, but...I've got a really bad feeling about Morgan, and no one will listen." Talking fast, she said, "It's like I'm watching my family, one by one, go under his spell. First Dad was sold, then you, and now Mom. It's like I'm all alone. I'm the only one who gets it."

"Gets what?" Jack would have asked more, but just then a giant shadow passed over them as if a cloud had covered the sun. Craning his neck, he saw a black shape soar past him, floating, wingtip feathers spread out like fingers. A condor! A condor had flown right over his head and into the gaping expanse of the Grand Canyon, sailing flawlessly on unseen currents of air.

"Oh my gosh—look how big it is!" Ashley screamed, instantly on her feet. "Hurry, get your camera! Somebody's got to call The Peregrine Fund people so they can catch him!"

Jack began to fumble with his case, his hands trembling as the mystic shape doubled back toward them. The big bird slowly glided toward the parking lot and disappeared between a row of cars. Jack and Ashley ran to see it, and they weren't the only ones. Every person along the rim seemed just as enchanted, streaming into the parking lot like water. By the time Jack reached the bird, the crowd had swelled to more than 70.

Now that he was up close, Jack could see the comical head of the condor—a yellow-gray bald head emerging from a choker of pin feathers. Bright-eyed and curious, the bird seemed as interested in the crowd as they were in him. Tags with the number 72 had been clipped to both wings, and Jack thought he could see a radio transmitter on the bird's tail. He began shooting film as quickly as he could, remembering what his father had said about quantity.

"Jack, should we get Mom?"

"Yeah. Can you do it, Ashley? I want to keep taking pictures in case The Peregrine Fund people show up to catch this guy. Mom and Morgan are just down the trail a little way."

"OK. I'll be right back!" Turning on her heel, she began to race down the path.

While the crowd pressed tighter, Jack circled the bird, shooting every second, stopping only to reload. Number 72 waddled toward a group of people who exclaimed in a language Jack didn't understand. It was amazing, seeing the bird this close. It stood over three feet tall, which was wondrous—he looked like a little old man hobbling along on a walk. What a strange, magnificent creature!

"Maybe he'd like to eat some of my peanuts," a

woman said, throwing a handful onto the ground.

"No! Don't feed him!" Jack protested. He ran to where the lady had tossed the nuts and began gathering them up. The asphalt felt rough beneath his fingertips. "The park rangers said that if you feed the condors, they have to stay in captivity. They must never associate people with food. It's really bad for them."

"Sorry," she answered, chastened. "Here, let me help." Her gray hair had been rolled into tight sausage curls that jiggled like a head full of bells as she bent down. Together, Jack and the woman picked up every last nut. Jack was just about to tell her more about the condors when he heard a sound that made his blood run cold. Every peanut he'd gathered spilled out of his hand as he began to run toward the rim, running faster than he ever had before.

The sound he'd heard was a scream. From Ashley.

CHAPTER EIGHT

Jack couldn't move fast enough as he bolted toward the rim of the canyon. He heard Ashley scream his name, over and over; it sent a cold terror through him that gripped his throat. Feet hammering against the pavement, he barely saw the path in front of him. He pushed his body as hard as he could, hurtling himself toward his sister's screams.

"Jack! Help! Jack!"

They were cries of terror. A sign pointing to Grandeur Point loomed ahead, and then he was there. Ashley stood rigid with fear. Morgan, shaking, peered over the rim. Olivia was nowhere to be seen.

"Jack—she's over the edge!" Ashley shrieked.

"Who?" Jack knew the answer, but he didn't want to hear it. The next words exploded into his mind like a grenade.

"Mom! Down there!"

Rushing to the rim, Jack wouldn't allow himself to even think what he might see. No one survived a fall down the sheer cliffs of the Grand Canyon. It was too deep, too sharp, too far. The absolute drop left no margin for error. If she'd gone over, she was dead.

"Where?" Jack demanded. *"Tell me exactly where!"*

Ashley pushed Morgan aside and dropped to her stomach. She pointed into a crevice of rock. "You can see her. She's not all the way down, but she's not moving!"

"Morgan, call 911!" Jack ordered.

"How?"

"Find someone with a cell phone! Go to a viewing station—I don't care how, *just do it!"*

In an instant, Morgan was gone.

Flinging himself down next to Ashley, Jack slid his body as far over the lip of the canyon as he dared. Rocks bit into his skin as he strained forward. He could see a part of his mother's legs protruding from a ledge 70 feet below. Most of her body was hidden by the branches of a stunted juniper tree, but Jack's eyes, like a camera lens, instantly recorded every detail that was visible: the pale blue cloth of her jeans, battered and covered with dirt and ripped open at the knees; her shoe—only one, the other one was missing; blood seeping into her sock, slowly turning the heel to crimson. There was not even a flicker of movement. Jack thought he would throw up—his heart hammered so hard in his chest that it wrenched against his stomach.

The same crowd that had been viewing the condor now panted up behind him, and he could hear a voice say, "Oh, my…I think someone fell!"

"To the bottom?"

"How horrible—"

"Call the police!"

"Let me see—"

"No!" Jack hadn't realized until then that he was crying. *"Stay away! Just stay away!"* But the crowd pressed forward to the edge before recoiling in horror. The woman with the gray hair put her hand to her mouth, shaking her head.

"Does anybody have a cell phone?" a man in the crowd demanded.

"I do, but mine doesn't work in the canyon," a young woman wearing a baseball cap cried out.

"I'll find a phone," a teenage boy said just as Morgan came running up, his face flushed, his hair whipped into dark strings. Breathlessly he gasped, "I called. They're—they're on their way. Does anybody know—like—first aid?"

The man who had asked for a cell phone shook his head. "None of us can help. Even if we could, there's no way to get down there. It's hopeless."

"Mom," Ashley cried desperately. "Mom! Are you OK? *Mom!*"

"Help's coming," Jack yelled down to his mother. "If you can hear me, move your leg, just a little. Can you hear me, Mom?" When Olivia's legs remained perfectly still, Jack tasted panic in his mouth. "Just hang on," he cried. "You're going to be all right!" His words disappeared into the vast chasm of the Grand Canyon.

After what seemed like an eternity, Jack heard a siren. Soon a paramedic unit arrived, brakes screeching as their vehicles drove straight along the asphalt hiking trail at the rim. "Everybody, clear out!" a man in a dark uniform barked. Others on the rescue team moved fast, unloading equipment from trucks.

"Get back from the edge, son," one of the Search and Rescue Team members told Jack. "Way back."

"It's my mother down there," Jack pleaded, but the man said, "Well, then, you certainly wouldn't want to hamper our rescue efforts, would you."

Another ranger was already herding Jack, Ashley, and Morgan back onto the paved path, where Jack, helpless, could do nothing but watch the procedure.

But he had no trouble hearing what they said. "She seems to be caught on the tree, but there's a chance it'll let loose, and she could fall all the way down."

"Set up a couple of anchors. There are some big boulders over there that'll hold weight." Within seconds, the team had wrapped ropes, separately, around each of the boulders.

"Equalize the weight," a woman ordered, pulling on the ropes. "Got the carabiners?"

"Right here." The man who'd first moved Jack out of

the way held up two large clamps with long ropes attached and offered, "I'll go down, Jenny. You belay me."

Almost before Jack could follow what was happening, the man, wearing a harness and holding a rope, had slipped over the edge of the cliff, while the woman named Jenny paid out a second rope to secure him. Less than a minute later, another member of the Search and Rescue Team lowered herself over the edge and began to rappel down the face of the cliff.

"They've reached the victim," a ranger said. "They've got a rescue harness on her." Jack had the feeling that the man was relaying that information for his and Ashley's benefit. "Now they're putting a cervical collar on her and getting her into a litter. We've got to start a line in her, and then we'll bring her up."

Cervical collar? That was one of those high stiff braces that protected an injured neck. If they were trying to protect Olivia's neck, that must mean she was— alive! Or was that just procedure? Why wouldn't they pull her up to the top so he could know for sure? Hurry, *hurry!* Jack cried under his breath, but time didn't move. Everything around him seemed slow motion.

Oblivious to the drama going on beneath them, a pair of hawks swooped close, curious to see what was happening below, but Jack felt only a surge of anger at their indifferent gaze. A lifetime ago he would have grabbed his camera and tried to get every shot he could of the birds riding the cool canyon breeze. But in a split second, nothing mattered that used to, not the birds or the shadows slicing the Grand Canyon with slashes of silver. All that mattered was strapped into a litter a hundred feet below.

"Here she comes," the man barked. "OK, people, stand back."

Just at that moment Steven reached them, his face red from exertion and panic. "I heard—" he gasped. "Is it…is it…?"

"Yes, it's Mom," Ashley cried, bursting into tears as she threw herself into her father's arms.

The woman, Jenny, who was working the belay line, asked Steven, "Are you the husband?"

"Yes—I'm Steven Landon. Olivia—my wife—is she…?"

"She's alive. I don't know anything about her condition, but she's still with us, and that's pretty much of a miracle."

With agonizing slowness, the team members pulled the litter up the side of the cliff.

"What's taking so long?" Ashley cried.

"We don't want to rush it," Jenny explained. "We need to take it slow to make sure she's safe. Don't worry, she's almost here. You need to stand back."

"Can you tell me anything about her condition?" Steven's voice sounded desperate.

"No. It's too soon. Please, sir, they're almost up. You need to stand back."

And then the litter appeared, and nothing could stop Steven and his two children from rushing forward. "Olivia!" he cried, and Jack and Ashley yelled, "Mom!"

"I'm sorry, you've got to back up, all of you," one of the rangers ordered. "We want to disconnect the rescue harness and get her into the ambulance. I know it's hard, but we're doing a job here."

His mother looked so small on the litter. The thick, white neck-brace dwarfed her face, which had been scraped raw on one side. Plastic tubes snaked from her arm, ending in a clear bag filled with some kind of fluid. It was her lifelessness that terrified Jack. If only she would make the tiniest flicker of motion. "Come on, Mom," he prayed under his breath. "Wake up." One of the paramedics gently pushed Jack out of the way, and he stood back where he'd been ordered to, watching. His fingernails dug into his palms, and his heart thumped wildly as he tried to reassure himself. His mother was alive, at least. Any minute now, she would wake up and everything would be the way it had been before.

One of the rangers was talking rapidly to Steven, filling him in on what had happened, on everything they'd done. "She got caught on that juniper tree on her way down," the man said. "That's what broke her fall. It kept her alive."

Jack watched as his father tightened an arm around Ashley while Morgan hovered behind them, nervously plucking at his meager beard, staring in silence.

"She looks so awful! What if she still might die?" Ashley sobbed.

Steven shook his head decisively. "That's not going to happen. She'll be all right." For a moment, Steven pulled his arm away from Ashley, pressed his fingers over his eyes, then, blinking hard, he opened them. "The most important thing is that she didn't go all the way down. That ledge, and the tree, saved her life."

The spot where Olivia had gone over the rim was the only place within a hundred-yard perimeter that had a ledge beneath it. And on that ledge grew a lone tree that had broken her fall, that had caught her in its branches like a mother's arms reaching out for a baby. Ten feet farther along the rim in either direction, east or west, would have meant a sheer, mile-long drop. And from that, there would have been no chance of survival.

"…apparent head injury and possible internal trauma," a paramedic called into a two-way radio. "Bruises and abrasions. BP is 86 over 64; pulse rate 122." There was a pause, and then, "OK. We're on our way."

"All right, people, let's move her," one of the paramedics ordered. "On my count: One, two, three…." The Search and Rescue Team moved back, and the paramedics hoisted the litter between them.

Olivia's feet swayed gently as the paramedics began

to carry her, but Jack thought he saw something else. A movement, so tiny it could have been made by butterfly wings, stirred on her face. "Wait!" he cried, rushing forward. "Her eyes—I think—!"

"Hold on!" The men carrying the litter stopped; one of the women paramedics squatted low, searching Olivia's face. "Ma'am, I'm Lisa Patrick with the Grand Canyon rescue team. You've had a fall. Can you hear me, ma'am?"

Like curtains parting, Olivia's lids fluttered open. It took a moment for her mouth to work, as if her lips were too stiff to form words properly.

"Steven?" she asked weakly.

"I'm here," Steven said, kneeling at her side, a look of relief and elation breaking across his face.

"Sir, please stand back for a moment." Lisa's voice was kind, but firm. "Ma'am, I'd like to ask you a few questions. What is your name?"

"Olivia." She swallowed, then added, "My name is Olivia Landon."

"Good. Can you tell me what day it is?"

"Tuesday," she said weakly. "I think—yes—it's Tuesday. I talked to CNN today. About the condors."

"Excellent. You're doing great. Olivia, you've had a fall. You went over the edge at Grandeur Point. Do you remember what happened?"

Raising her arm, Olivia gingerly touched her neck. "I'm in a brace?"

"Yes. I'd like to ask you not to move your head until we get you checked out. We need some x-rays. Can you wiggle your hands for me?"

Olivia's hands clenched and unclenched, and Jack felt a sudden surge of joy. He wasn't a doctor, but he knew that being able to move was a good sign.

His mother spoke again, and this time her voice was urgent. "Jack—Ashley?"

"I'm right here," Jack answered, while Ashley gave a worried smile and asked, "Do you hurt, Mom?"

"Morgan...? Where's Morgan?"

"Here. Man, you just disappeared," Morgan said. His voice sounded strangely tight, as if he had to push each syllable from his throat. "I mean, first you were there, and then you weren't."

"Yes...I remember...."

"All right, Olivia, we have to get you to the medical center," Lisa insisted, rolling back onto her heels and standing up. "Mr. Landon, you can ride in the ambulance with us, but I'm afraid there's not enough room for your children. If it's all right with you, they can go with Ranger Kenton here and meet up with us at the Grand Canyon Clinic."

A man in a park uniform stepped forward. His skin was dark, and he was square-jawed. Thick muscles rippled beneath his taut shirt. In a deep, rumbling voice he announced, "I'm Ted Kenton, a law-enforcement ranger here at the park." To Lisa, he said, "I'd be happy to bring the kids. But before you take Dr. Landon, I have one question I need to ask." Placing himself directly in her line of vision, he inquired, "Do you remember what happened to you, Dr. Landon?"

"Yes." Olivia touched her neck brace again. "I… I was standing. At the rim. But not too close."

"Not too close?" Ranger Kenton's eyes widened. He looked as if he were from the military, holding himself in a way that elevated every millimeter of his five-foot-ten-inch height. Something about what she said seemed to have caught his concern. "Right. Not too close. Watching a condor."

"Ted, is this necessary? Can't you wait?" Lisa interrupted. "We should take her for x-rays."

"Just one more minute," he said, holding up his hand. "Were you alone?"

Olivia's face clouded as she attempted to remember. "Morgan was gone. There was nobody around. I called to him to see the condor, but…." Her voice drifted off.

"Did you slip, Dr. Landon? Was the gravel under your feet loose? Were you trying to climb down?"

"No." Her eyebrows wrinkled in concentration and she cried, "I'm sure of—I heard footsteps. From behind."

"Footsteps?" Ranger Kenton's face was unreadable, but he began writing in a notepad.

"Yes. Fast. Running, maybe. I thought it was Morgan…."

"Olivia, you don't need to…" Steven began, touching the side of her cheek with his fingertips. But she clutched his hand so tightly he asked, "What is it? What's wrong, Olivia?"

Olivia's eyes had widened so that Jack could see the whites all around. "I remember—I remember going over the edge!"

"But you're OK now," Steven said soothingly, shooting Lisa a worried look. "Can we finish this later?" he asked Ranger Kenton. "This is obviously upsetting her."

"No!" Olivia cried. "I want to say it. There was a smell. Strong. Like—kerosene."

"What else do you remember, Dr. Landon?" Ranger Kenton asked, bending close.

"I felt something slam into my back." Suddenly, Olivia looked as though she could connect her thoughts with perfect, frightening clarity. "I didn't slip. I didn't fall. *Someone pushed me!"*

CHAPTER NINE

It took a moment for his mother's statement to register.

"Someone pushed me!" Olivia cried again.

The words seemed to slow time, as if every frame of Jack's life hung suspended between the seconds. His mother hadn't slipped. She'd been pushed. The ravens suddenly appeared again, their cries mocking as they soared in slow circles, black wings cutting the air like scythes in a sky that looked as though water and air had merged into a deep blue glass. Someone had tried to kill his mother. It was impossible to comprehend.

Ranger Ted Kenton's face became grave. "Do you know who could have done this?"

"No!" Olivia began to tremble as Steven rubbed her arm soothingly.

"We got a threatening e-mail. Someone said my wife deserved to die—I should have stayed with her," Steven said, choking up.

"I heard running…and then…" Olivia moaned.

"Ted, you've got to let me take her to the clinic," Lisa broke in. "Her pulse rate is going up, and we must get those x-rays. I'll have to ask you to do this later."

"Yes, of course." Ted nodded tersely. "But I'll need that e-mail and the laptop."

"I already took it to the park police office. That's where I was when this happened," Steven answered.

Snapping his notebook shut, Ranger Kenton said, "I realize all of this is extremely difficult for you, but I would like to talk to these children."

"Now?" Steven asked, somewhat surprised.

"Yes, while the information is still fresh. I'll bring them to the clinic as soon as I'm done. Since they're minors, I need your permission to question them. Are all of them yours?" He looked from Jack to Morgan.

"I'm not," Morgan answered. His eyes turned a cold, wintry gray, but no one but Jack seem to notice.

"Morgan is a temporary foster child," Steven explained to Ted. "It's not a problem—I have legal authority over him. You have my permission." Then he turned his attention to Olivia.

"On three!" Lisa commanded. The paramedics hoisted the litter up to knee height.

"But I want to go with Mom!" Ashley wailed.

Ted Kenton said, "There's nothing you can do to help your mother." He ushered the three of them to one side as the paramedics carried the stretcher to the ambulance. Holding a transmitter close to his lips, he said, "Dispatch...541. I'm at Grandeur Point, and I'll be needing backup for investigation of a possible crime scene. I'll keep the area clear until backup arrives." He listened for a minute, then said, "Check if Rex Tilousi is in the area and send him down—he's got a good eye. I have three juvenile witnesses I'm going to talk to—541 clear." Shutting off the transmitter, Ted turned his gaze on the three kids. "So," he said calmly. "Why don't you tell me what happened."

"I don't know. I wasn't here when she fell," Ashley answered, trembling. "But Morgan was."

"Try to think back and tell me exactly what went on. Can you do that for me?"

Ashley swallowed, hard. "When I got to the rim, Morgan was standing right there, looking over. He was all white—he was really scared when he saw me. He said...." She took a wavering breath as a tear spilled down her cheek to land softly on the shoulder of her jacket. "He said my mom was gone. And then he—he pointed down there! I started screaming for Jack."

Ted looked at Morgan sharply, but continued to speak to Ashley. "Where were you before that?"

"In the parking lot. There was a condor. Number 72."

A condor? Jack realized how fragmented his thinking had become. Had the condor been today? It seemed as though a lifetime had elapsed since then.

Now Ted turned to Jack. "What about you, son?"

Jack tried to focus his mind. What had he witnessed? Ashley, screaming. Morgan running to call 911. His mother's twisted legs. Shards of images that were hard for him to piece together, all of them jumbled though the visual lens of his memory. The crowd. The paramedics. The rescue. If there was one thing he could remember with certainty, it was that except for Morgan and Ashley, the rim had been completely deserted.

"I heard Ashley scream, and then I saw Morgan, just like my sister said. That's all I know."

"Did you see anyone else when you ran down the trail? A man, maybe? Or a woman?"

"No one else was here."

"Morgan?" Ranger Kenton turned toward him.

Jack watched Morgan tense. His question-mark posture straightened as he dug his hands deep into his pockets and asked, "What?"

"I'd like to hear your side."

"What do you mean, my 'side?'"

Ranger Kenton flipped a page of his notepad to a fresh sheet. He clicked his pen and replied, "You are the closest thing I have to an eyewitness. You were the only other person at the rim at the time of the incident."

"Me and whoever pushed her over."

"Exactly. So, what happened?" When Morgan didn't answer, Ted Kenton moved closer. "Do you have a problem with that question?"

"No. I just don't like how you're asking it." Morgan's

voice was even, but his face had gone hard. This must be the side of himself Morgan had shown in Dry Creek—stubborn, resistant, wary.

The next words out of Ted Kenton's mouth were nothing short of a command. "Tell me."

"I was gone for a few minutes. I came back. Mrs. Landon had disappeared. I called for her, but she didn't answer. I started looking around. I went up the path, then came back to the rim. I looked over the edge and saw her legs sticking out. Right after that Ashley showed up. She yelled for Jack, and you know the rest."

"Go back to the statement, 'I was gone for a few minutes.' Where did you go?"

Morgan flushed. "Away."

"Before you left, did you see anyone else? Tourists snapping pictures? Anyone walking around?"

Morgan shook his head and touched his goatee.

"How close to the edge would you say Dr. Landon was standing? Before you left, I mean."

Morgan shrugged. "Maybe about three feet."

"So where did you go?" Ted Kenton persisted.

"I already told you. For a walk in the trees. Over there." Morgan swept his arm out to the left, toward a cluster of pines.

"May I ask why?"

"No, you may not." Morgan thrust out his chin, refusing to say more. Jack could tell that the ranger was growing impatient.

"Hey, cut the attitude," Kenton demanded.

"I was the last one there, right? She was pushed. It's all implied—I must be the one who pushed her. Just like Dry Creek, guilty without a trial." Eyes narrowing into slits, Morgan spat, "By the way, I've spent a lot of time learning my legal rights. You need parental consent to even question me, and you haven't got it."

"Whoa, whoa, *whoa!*" Ted Kenton's hands pressed into the air, as though he were pushing back an invisible wall. "Hold on. I'm asking you to explain why you went into the trees. There's no need to be so defensive."

Sighing, Morgan closed his eyes. It seemed as though he were waging an internal argument, one that played out through his expressions. Finally, he blurted out, blushing, "All right. I was in need of a bathroom, OK? I knew Dr. Landon would freak if I went 'natural'—so I waited until she was busy looking for that condor. Then I used a tree. I came back, and she was gone. That's it."

"But that's not *all* of it." Ashley said, her voice sharp. "Tell him about your Web site and the bad things you wrote about Mom and me!"

"Ashley!" Jack cried, but his sister vehemently shook her head. "No, I should never have listened to you. If anyone had believed me, this wouldn't have happened! Ranger Kenton, my mom and Morgan were fighting."

Ted zeroed in on every word. "Fighting, like physical fighting? Or fighting with words."

"Words."

"Aw, man, *we were taking a walk together!*" Morgan protested.

"That's because you had won her over," Ashley sputtered. "Like you did Dad. And Jack. But not *me!*"

An expression of anger mixed with panic twisted Morgan's face as he turned to the ranger. "Forget what she said. Ask Jack. He'll tell you I didn't do it. Go on," Morgan demanded, "ask him!"

"I'm only interested in facts," Kenton answered. "Ashley, I promise I'll look into the e-mail business. Morgan," he said, pointing his finger at Morgan's chest, "if I hear even a hint of retaliation against this girl, I will haul you in so fast—do you understand?"

"I understand everything."

Abruptly, Ted looked over Morgan's head to wave at a figure approaching them from behind. "Rex—over here!"

Jack turned to see a rather small Native American man approaching them. Salt-and-pepper hair hung down his shoulders in thin braids, and his weathered skin broke into a thousand wrinkles when he smiled. His uniform seemed softer than the other rangers', as if it were a comfortable skin that moved easily with him. His leather boots were scarred and the tips dusty. When he spoke, his voice sounded warm and even. "I hear things went well today. A life saved. A blessing."

"Yes. But Dr. Landon believes she was pushed,"

Ted added bluntly. He led the way to the spot where the rescue had taken place. "I took a cursory look, but nothing popped out. Can you give it a try? You kids stay here."

Rex made his way to the very edge of the rim and stared intently at the ground. Jack and Morgan hung back under a knot of trees, waiting for any clues to be sifted from the earth. Ashley went farther away and sat by herself, her back toward Jack, arms wrapped tightly around her legs, and her chin resting on top of her knees. The breeze ruffled her hair so that it moved like dark water.

"She's pretty upset," Jack stated.

"I'm the one who should be mad," Morgan declared hotly. "She said...."

"I know what she said. I also know why she said it."

"Yeah...well...." Shoving his fists into his pockets, Morgan went to where Ted had begun to tape off the area with bright yellow plastic ribbon printed with Crime Scene—Do Not Cross. Jack drifted toward it as well. He could hear Rex talking in his slow, even way.

"The ledge is rocky, and those here for the rescue stirred the earth. The edge reveals little."

Ted sighed. "Anything else?"

"I found this juniper twig. It was at the point Dr. Landon fell." Holding up a plastic bag with a small bit of green inside, Rex said, "Look close, and you can see this twig has been broken. The edge is sharp. The person you seek may have been waiting in a stand of trees."

"You mean someone could have been hiding in there, so as not to be seen?"

Rex nodded. "Or it could have come from one of the paramedics, or even Dr. Landon herself. To push a person over the edge can be a perfect crime."

"Thanks for looking, Rex. I would have missed this twig, and it could be significant. We'll send it to the lab to look for fiber evidence."

When Ted suddenly caught sight of Jack, he spoke to Rex quickly and then hurried over to the kids.

"Change of plans. I'm pretty tied up here. Would you guys mind if Rex took you to the clinic?"

"I just want to get there," Jack answered.

"Bring your sister and your friend," Rex said gently. "And follow me."

#

The clinic smelled clean. Two green love seats and an assortment of chairs filled the tiny waiting room. A coffee table, stacked with worn NATIONAL GEOGRAPHIC magazines, had been set squarely in the center. Small ferns sprayed from the corners in hammocks of braided macrame, like emerald waterfalls. Jack went directly to the receptionist, who looked up at him placidly. "May I help you?" she asked.

"I'm Jack Landon, and I'd like to see my mother, Olivia Landon."

The receptionist, whose name tag said Marie Ophan, was rounder than most of the people at the park. Her pale eyes looked at Jack from behind wire-framed glasses, which were resting halfway down her nose. "Oh yes, the miracle lady," she said, breaking into a smile. "She's in the back, getting x-rayed."

"I—we'd like to see her."

"Oh, I don't know about that. There's not enough room back there for the four of you."

"I won't be staying," Rex told her. "Just the children."

Marie made a clicking sound with her lips. "Why don't you all have a seat while I find out what's going on. I will say this—not many people fall into the Grand Canyon like that and live to tell about it!"

Jack nodded woodenly.

"Come and sit down," Rex suggested, leading them toward the chairs. "I will stay with you for now—until you get settled."

Marie bustled off to the back, leaving the front room of the clinic completely empty.

"You don't have to wait around," Jack told Rex, dropping into one of the chairs. The fabric felt rough against his skin. Shifting uncomfortably, he said, "I'm sure you've got other things to do."

"No," Rex said simply. "I will stay."

Suit yourself, Jack said in his mind. All he wanted now was to get this day over with and start another one. He tapped his foot on the floor. The rubber sole of his sneaker didn't make much of a sound, just a soft *thump, thump, thump,* like a dog's hind leg when you scratch its sweet spot. Ashley took the band out of her pony tail, re-smoothed her hair, then rebanded it. She hadn't spoken since she'd entered the car, and Rex, too, didn't appear to feel the need to talk. Face placid, he rested his hands on his knees and looked straight ahead while Morgan hung around the work station, staring at the computer screen.

"Are you a Hopi?" Ashley asked Rex.

"I'm Havasupai."

"Really? Aren't they the ones who live in the Grand Canyon—I mean, way down there, at the bottom?"

"My people do. I stay above, in a village close to headquarters. I'm an interpretive ranger for the park."

"Oh," Ashley said, and after that the conversation seemed to dry up. Ashley practically jumped out of her seat when Marie returned to the waiting-room area, a smile pushing her cheeks into doughy balls. "Well, I've got some good news," she told them brightly. "Your mother is fine. But they are doing x-rays, so the doctor doesn't want anyone in there until he's finished."

"Pardon me, ma'am?" Morgan asked loudly. "Are you connected to the Internet? I desperately need to check something online."

"Our computers are for staff only. Now if you'll excuse me, I'm needed in back." She hurried out of the reception area, swinging the door behind her.

Rex looked puzzled. "Why does the boy need the Internet?"

"He's a computer geek," Ashley explained without looking at Morgan.

"My grandchildren are the same way. They let their spirits be taken over by the speed of that world. Now they have no time to listen, to hear from us elders, to discover our stories. A computer is like a thief who steals our children." He stopped speaking as quickly as he'd started. Morgan, though, had heard every word. He stomped to where Rex sat and demanded, "Have you ever been on the Net?"

"No," Rex answered pleasantly.

"Then how can you say it's 'stealing' our children? You don't know what you're talking about."

"Anything that takes minds away from the old ways creates a loss. I am an elder of my people, yet even my own grandchildren do not know the stories. They want things that flash. They do not care for what was, for what we know."

"Do you have a story about the condor?" Ashley asked quickly. Jack guessed that she wanted to keep Morgan from arguing with Rex. Or maybe she just didn't didn't want to hear any more from Morgan.

Rex seemed to hesitate. "It is a sacred thing to share these traditions."

"Maybe a legend that your grandchildren should hear? Tell us about the condor," Ashley pleaded. "My mom is trying to save them. That's what brought her here, to the Grand Canyon. If you tell me, I'll pass it on to her."

The leathery skin on Rex's face softened as he looked into Ashley's eager eyes. Settling into his chair, he nodded. Then he began to speak.

Our stories tell of when creation first began. A big bird, a condor, put my people on its wings so that they could take flight into the air. The condor's flight began from down at the bottom of the canyon, where the springs are, where the waters are, where the waterfalls are, and as it flew to the top, songs were created. When the wings of the condor tipped the red walls, there was a song. As that great bird came above to the higher rims, the wings tipped the white walls, and another song was born. When the wings tipped the cliffs, the ages of the wall became a song. A song we sing to my people.

And as the great bird flew up above the rim, it took to the west, where the Walapai live, down to where the Mahapai live, on to the north where the Paiute live, farther north, where the Kahaback Paiute live, over the east where the San Juan Paiute live and the Hopi and Navajo, where the natives live out to the east, and on around over to the south, where the Yavapai live and the Kwichan, and over onto the west where Walipai Mohavi live. It is said this bird made a big circle around the sacred canyon, in what you would call a halo, and then it flew back into the canyon and landed right where it began. We still dance to those songs, which we call the round dance. Now, as we stand and look down into the canyon, the Havasupai see the many colors that live here on the Earth. The rocks, the red rocks, the water, the color of those waters, the four colors of people that live here and under the Earth. You see the painted desert out there, all kinds of shades that make up Mother Earth. The song I'm speaking of goes like this.

Rex closed his eyes and began a chant with words Jack could not comprehend, and yet, somehow, the understanding didn't matter. Staccato rhythms seemed to carry Jack back in time to where a condor soared through the red rock with the Havasupai riding on two enormous black wings. Hauntingly beautiful, the chant was over as quickly as it had begun.

Rex slowly opened his eyes. 'Those who believe in the spiritual way of life and who follow the spiritual path, those people are sacred." His eyes flickered over to Morgan, who looked quickly away. And yet, Jack could tell Morgan was impressed. It was the set of his face—quiet, for once, and thoughtful.

"There is power in that circle," Rex went on. "Right now, the circle is not complete. We have stepped away, because of the many things that we see around us. The computers, the televisions, the new inventions that we have, all those keep people out of that circle."

Resting his hands on his knees, he said, "We need to step forward and join hands, and we will be brought back into that circle. That is my wish."

All of a sudden, Marie's cheerful voice rang out, startling Jack. "You can come back now!" Jack hadn't even heard Marie come through the swinging door, yet here she was, her large shape looming in his line of sight.

"I will go, then," Rex said, rising.

"Thank you so much, Mr. Tilousi," Ashley told him, placing her hand in his. "I loved your story."

"Yeah, it was great," Jack agreed. "Really."

Rex nodded but said nothing to them. His dark eyes rested on Morgan's face. This time Morgan didn't look away, but returned the gaze.

"OK, the thing is, you don't have to give up one world to visit another," Morgan told Rex quickly. "I need to get on the Net for a reason. But I can't work without tools. The Net is my hands and my feet and my eyes and all my senses. It's my mind."

"But not your soul," Rex told him.

"Right. Maybe there *are* things that don't come from the wired world. I can admit to that. But maybe you can admit the opposite—that good things can come from my world, too."

Smiling quietly, Rex made his way toward the glass door. "Perhaps we all must learn," he said. Then he was gone.

CHAPTER TEN

"**H**ey now, don't worry, I'll be fine," Olivia told her family as they pressed close around her bedside. "They just want me to get a little rest, that's all."

After visiting with Olivia for an hour, the Landons and Morgan had just been told by the clinic doctor—a compact man who was bald except for a feeble ponytail at the back of his neck—that it would be best if they left now. Jack could believe it. With the purple-red scrape on the side of his mother's face and her foot wrapped and elevated, Olivia did look as though she needed time to heal. But Ashley was resisting.

"Why can't you come with us now, Mom?" she asked, a quaver in her voice. "Are you hurt worse than you're telling me?"

Steven began, "No, Ashley, she's going to be fine." Then, noticing Ashley's frightened expression, he sat down and pulled her toward him, saying, "Look in my eyes, sweetie. You believe that I'm telling the truth, don't you? When people have a head injury, the doctors like to observe them at least overnight to make sure there are no serious problems—it's just procedure. But we really have to go now."

As the four of them left the clinic, Jack couldn't help being amazed by the stars that blazed from the blackness. A cloud drifted across the half-moon, deepening the darkness before moving on. The cool canyon breeze made him shiver so that he wrapped his arms around himself tight, rubbing his shoulders for warmth.

They stopped at the cafeteria to pick up a couple of sandwiches to take back to the rooms, but no one was very hungry. With their still-wrapped sandwiches in their hands, Jack and Morgan paused in the hall of the lodge while Jack fumbled in his pocket for the plastic card that would unlock the door. As soon as he opened the door, Steven entered the room right behind the two boys and announced, "We're changing things tonight. Jack, you and Ashley will sleep next door in the room where your mother and I were. I'll stay over here with Morgan."

Morgan straightened as though his spine had suddenly been electrified. "Why?" he demanded, then answered his own question. "You want to keep watch over me because you think I'll run away." Like a trapped animal, Morgan stood with his back flattened against the wall, his eyes wide.

Steven said nothing.

"So I'm judged guilty without a trial. You're going to turn me in, aren't you?"

"Morgan, calm down," Steven told him. "You're not being arrested. You're just not going to be left alone." Steven fastened the chain lock on the door that led to the hall, then turned to face Morgan. "I want you to take a look at yourself through everyone else's eyes. You're the boy who trashed people on a nasty Web site, and yes, the park law-enforcement rangers found out about that. You're a computer whiz who flamed my wife and daughter. You knew Olivia was thinking about sending you back, which they consider a motive. Olivia received an anonymous threat by e-mail, and you're one of the only people around here knowledgeable enough to do that. You were with her on the rim of the canyon, but you say you weren't really there when she went over the edge. It looks bad."

"But I didn't do anything!" Morgan yelled. "I'm telling the truth."

"I believe you. But it's not too hard to figure out why people are suspicious." Steven looked suddenly weary. "There's an old saying that you should think about. You 'reap what you sow.'" Sighing loudly, he said, "OK, Jack, grab your toothbrush and your sleep clothes and get over to the other room with Ashley. After you're in there, latch the door from your side. Take your mother's laptop with you."

Morgan said bitterly, "So you're locking me up for the night. I'm a prisoner. And you're the guard."

"If you want to think of it that way, fine," Steven said. "It won't change anything."

Jack did as his father had instructed him, although the whole situation made him uneasy. He could only guess at the frustration Morgan must be feeling.

"You really believe him?" Ashley asked as she kicked off her shoes.

"Yeah," Jack answered. "Morgan's weird, but he's not a murderer."

"How do you know?"

"How does anyone know anything? What did he say to you at the rim?"

"He said he was sorry about the stuff he wrote about me. He wanted me to give him a chance to prove that he was innocent. He said he'd always fought his battles with words, and that he'd never hurt anything in his life."

"What did you say?"

"I said, 'Having awful things written about you can hurt worse than being hit.' And then he said, 'I guess I know that now,' and I said,'I'm not like the rest of my family. I don't trust you. Just stay away from me, and I'll stay away from you.'"

"Real nice," Jack snapped at her, but then he felt immediately sorry as Ashley's eyes filled with tears. "Listen, I'll turn on the TV, and we can watch a program while we fall asleep," he offered, picking up the remote control. But the first thing to appear on the television screen was an image of their mother standing on the rim of the Grand Canyon.

"...interviewed earlier today," the reporter's voice was saying. "Hours later, Dr. Landon fell over the edge of the Grand Canyon not far from the very spot where she'd made her plea against Cash-for-Carcasses hunts and lead-pellet shotgun shells. Miraculously, Dr. Landon survived; her fall was broken by a juniper tree growing on a ledge beneath the rim. CNN has learned that Dr. Landon believes someone pushed her over the edge. We'll have more on this breaking story as it unfolds. Back to you, Paula."

"Turn the channel! I don't want to see anymore."

Jack flipped through the TV channels until he found a cartoon network. Ashley crawled into her mother's bed and pulled the pillow around her head. "I can smell Mom's shampoo on this pillow." She sounded like she might start to cry again.

"Mom will be back with us tomorrow," Jack assured her.

A smell on the pillow. What Ashley had just said started Jack's thoughts whirring in his head. Right after his mother had been rescued, she'd mentioned something about a smell. "Like kerosene," she'd told the ranger. Jack had been with Morgan nearly all the time until Olivia had gone over the edge, and Morgan certainly hadn't smelled like kerosene. If anything, he'd smelled like the pizza he'd dropped on his shirt earlier that afternoon in the cafeteria. It had made quite a mess on his shirtfront.

Except for the glow of the television screen, the room was dark. After he was certain that Ashley had fallen asleep, Jack got up and opened his mother's laptop computer. He didn't need to connect it to the telephone line to bring up her e-mail—once e-mail was received, it was stored in the computer. There it was. The threat.

DR LANDON
YOU THINK VARMITS DESERV TO LIVE. YOUR WRONG. DEAD WRONG. VARMITS DESERV TO DIE. AND SO DO YOU.

It just didn't sound like Morgan. Morgan was a smart guy—he'd certainly know how to spell "deserve." And "you're" and "varmints." Unless, of course, he'd been trying to make the message *look* as though it came from someone who couldn't spell.

Troubled, Jack turned off the laptop, quietly closed the lid, and hit the remote button to shut down the TV. He didn't expect to sleep much, but he did. He was dead to the world when Ashley pounded his shoulder and said, "Wake up. I hear Dad and Morgan moving around in the next room."

Squinting through half-closed eyelids, Jack could see that it was morning. And not too early in the morning, from the looks of the sun shining through the window.

He could hear voices now, too—his father and Morgan, arguing once more. Unlocking the door that connected the two rooms, Jack peered in and said, "Hi."

"Get dressed," his father told him brusquely. "Tell Ashley to get dressed too."

Morgan was saying, "I'm not finished giving you my reasons, if you'd just listen. This is the United States of America. A man is presumed to be innocent until he's proved guilty. And I can prove I'm *innocent.*"

In a tone of voice Jack recognized as meaning no more arguments allowed, his father answered, "We are going to have breakfast, and then we're going to the clinic to see Olivia. That's *all* we're going to do."

Since Morgan didn't know Steven well enough to understand what that particular tone meant, he kept right on arguing. "All I need is a couple of hours on Olivia's computer, and I can nail that jerk who sent the threat. Maybe not even a couple of hours. Maybe less than that if I can—"

"Morgan!"

Jack beat a hasty retreat. Forget about a shower, he told himself, throwing on his clothes. "Ashley, move it!" he yelled. "Dad's in a mood."

Jack was surprised when Morgan wolfed down two huge stacks of pancakes at breakfast. He'd read a phrase once, something about 'the condemned man ate a hearty meal.' Morgan wasn't acting like a condemned man; he looked like a guy with a plan. And an appetite.

At the clinic, they crowded around the chair where Olivia was sitting, still wearing a hospital gown, her foot with the bandaged heel elevated on a little stool. The abrasion on her face looked nasty, even worse than the bruises on her arms and legs. "They won't let me go yet," she said, smiling ruefully. "Since this whole thing has turned into a police matter, I have to stay here for more physical exams and more interviews with the law-enforcement people."

"How much longer?" Ashley wanted to know, twining her fingers through her mother's.

"Maybe two more hours," Olivia answered, and Morgan interrupted, "That's all I'd need!"

When Olivia looked inquiringly, Steven said, "Let it go, Olivia. Don't get him started."

"No, what is it? Tell me," Olivia urged.

It was Morgan who spilled it all out, talking non-stop. He was sure, he told Olivia, that if he could just use her laptop, he could find the person who'd sent the threatening e-mail. And that person was probably the one who'd pushed her off the cliff.

"But they said there was no way to trace it."

"For them, no. But I think I can. At least let me try," he insisted. "It's not fair that everyone thinks I did it, and no one will give me a chance to prove that I didn't. And there's one more thing nobody seems to be thinking of here."

"What's that?" Olivia asked.

"Just this: Whoever really did do this to you is still out there. I mean, have you considered what will happen if he comes looking for you again? If you don't let me find him…." Morgan let his sentence hang in the air. He didn't have to finish it.

"Is that true, Mom?" Ashley asked, eyes wide.

Jack's throat tightened. "Last night, on the news, they announced you were alive. That means the man who did this will know he didn't get you!"

"Now don't panic, kids. Ranger Kenton feels I'm not in any danger since no one knows where I am. He even told the reporters I was recovering in a clinic in Flagstaff. I'm perfectly safe."

Morgan grabbed Olivia's hand. "Dr. Landon—Olivia—help me clear my name. Let me use your computer. Let me find who really did this. Please."

Jack held his breath as he waited for his mother to answer. "OK," Olivia said slowly. "I don't see where we lose in this. You do what you have to do, Morgan."

"But Olivia," Steven objected, "we can't hook up to the Internet here in the clinic. That means I'll have to stay in the room at the lodge with Morgan for the next couple of hours while he chases electronic rabbits."

"Do you know why Mr. Landon doesn't want to let me do it?" Morgan chimed in, directing it to Olivia. "Because he doesn't believe a computer geek like me can crack a case better than a squad of detectives. He thinks he'll be wasting his time."

"Yes, you've got that right," Steven agreed through tight lips. "I'd much rather stay here with my wife. I don't want to leave her alone. Even for a minute."

Olivia said, "Steven, this could be really important. Besides, Ashley will be here to keep me company, and there's a nurse, a doctor, and a receptionist hanging around. Morgan's a pretty smart guy. I'd like to have him working on my side. And Morgan—"

Morgan was already at the door, leaning against the door frame. He turned back to say, "Yeah?"

"When you're online, I want you to ask Snipe to send you a list of where the Cash-for-Carcasses checkpoints are located in the state of Arizona."

"Why?"

"Just humor me. I've got a portable printer in my suitcase. Steven will give it to you, and then I'd like a hard copy. Will you do it?"

He grinned at her. "Yeah, I'll do it."

Once back at the room in the lodge, Morgan set up the laptop and began to make his connections. First, he "talked" to Snipe as Jack and Steven stood behind him, watching. When the printer cable was connected, Morgan pushed a button, and three sheets of paper shot through the printer before it beeped, signaling an end to the list. "Here's this," Morgan said, handing the papers to Steven. "Now for the good stuff."

"Can you tell me just what you're planning to do, exactly?" Steven inquired.

"Well, see," Morgan told them, without pausing for even a moment, "if a guy wants to send an e-mail so that no one knows who it's from, he goes to an anonymous remailer."

"What's that?" Jack asked.

"It's someone who sets up a system where they receive an e-mail, then they strip the sender's name and any identification from the message. The remailer sends it out again under some made-up alias that's not gonna be traced back to the original sender."

"Why didn't park law-enforcement officers know about this?"

Morgan snorted. "Hardly anyone knows how to do it. You've got to be really wired to find this."

"So what are you doing now?" Steven asked him.

"I'm contacting all my online friends. There are dozens of anonymous remailers out there, and I can't hack into all of them by myself. I need help."

"Wait!" Steven grabbed Morgan by the shoulders. "I just heard you say 'hack.' That's illegal, isn't it?"

Morgan turned to face him. "Not when the FBI does it. The FBI uses a system called Carnivore to spy on the e-mail of U.S. citizens."

"You're *not* the FBI," Steven told him.

"No, I'm not." Morgan pushed back the chair, looked up at Steven, and stared defiantly into his eyes. "You can call the FBI if you want to. They'll investigate this threat to your wife—when they get around to it, which means when they have enough people to put on this case. Like, maybe, in a couple of weeks. In the meantime, this crazy guy who sent the threat and probably pushed your wife off the cliff has time to come back and try again." Slowly, Morgan folded his arms across his chest. "Or—you can let me and my friends do it. And you'll find out right away. It's your call, man."

Steven's jaw worked as he contemplated Morgan, who sat before him as if he didn't really care which way Steven decided. But Jack knew that was all a bluff. Morgan wanted desperately to discover who had sent the e-mail.

At last, quietly, Steven said, "Get him."

Morgan pumped his fist, and with a grin that spread all across his face, whispered, *"Yes!"* Then he turned to Jack and said, "Pull up some chairs, this is about to get interesting."

Morgan would make a great teacher, Jack thought. Even though he stayed focused on whatever it was he was doing on the computer, he also kept up a running commentary, explaining everything to Jack. "What's happening now is, I'm sending e-mails to all my gaming partners, telling them what I need. Each of us will hack into about three or four anonymous remailer systems to look for the e-mail your mother got. Then we'll know which one sent it. It's tricky, because usually an anonymous e-mail goes from one remailer to another several times. Each one strips off identification from the message before he relays it the next time, so it can't be traced backward."

"You mean—maybe you won't be able to trace it after all?" Jack asked, disappointed.

"Hey, you're dealin' with the pros here," Morgan bragged. "We'll nail this jerk to the wall. Two things we know—the size of the message and when it was sent. They're like fingerprints. That's what we look for."

Words flashed on and off the screen so fast Jack had trouble reading them. "The guy probably used the cheapest anonymous remailer he could find to send the threat," Morgan was saying, "which means it got relayed through only a couple of systems. At least, that's my guess. The more security steps the message goes through—meaning the more times it gets relayed—the harder it is to trace, and the more it costs the sender. I figure this guy was either too stupid or too cheap to do it the complicated way, with lots of relays, plus encryption." Morgan shot a glance at Jack. "Encryption means turning the message into codes so no one can read it."

"I know that," Jack said.

An hour passed. Then another quarter hour, and all the while Morgan kept chattering like a magpie. "I ran a port scanner to find out what services are running. Now I'm looking for documented security holes or exploits in those services. I'm getting user access—if the FTP daemon e-mails me the password, I'll be able to crack the file, then do a reverse e-mail."

Morgan might have been speaking in Swahili for all Jack understood. His father looked just as lost.

At last Morgan's face lit up. "And there he is. Well, well, well. I *told* you I didn't send this. I wish Ashley were here. This proves beyond a shadow of a doubt that I am innocent! Free at last!"

"Who wrote it?" Steven demanded.

"A man named Thornton Rawlings sent the e-mail. He paid for it with a credit card. We hacked into the credit card records and found out where the guy lives— it's a little town about 25 miles from here, easy enough for him to come over here and try to kill your wife. She announced on national television where she was going to be all day. The rest is simple."

Jack sucked in his breath. Morgan was amazing! Steven's face showed conflicting emotions—relief, then respect, replaced by doubt.

"What?" Jack asked his father.

"We've got a problem," Steven said. "None of this proves this guy came over to the park and actually pushed Olivia."

"What do you mean? He threatened her!" Morgan pointed to the screen and cried, "It's there in black and white!"

"All I'm saying is that the police will need more evidence to place Rawlings physically at the rim."

Slamming his fist into his thigh, Morgan complained,

"So giving them a name isn't enough, is that what you're saying? They'll still think it could be me!"

"We'll give Rawlings' name to them, of course, but it won't place him at the scene. It's not over, Morgan."

Morgan raked his fingers across his scalp, leaving dark corn rows of hair. "Great. Well, I've done all I can do. My trail ends here."

Steven rubbed his chin with his hand and looked off in the distance. Thoughts nagged Jack one after another as he tried to snag the idea that seemed to nibble right at the edges. There was something he was missing. Why couldn't he see it? Suddenly, he jumped up from the chair so fast he knocked it backwards. "Wait, maybe we *can* prove he was here," he cried excitedly. "When the condor landed in the parking lot, it came down right in the middle of a whole bunch of parked cars and trucks and SUVs. The condor kept moving, and *I* kept running around it so I could take its picture from a lot of different angles. There's maybe a hundred license plates that will show up on the pictures I took. There's got to be a way to check those out. If we can show he was there—"

"Where's the film?" Steven asked.

"It's still in my camera. We can find the nearest one-hour photo place—maybe there's one here in the park—"

"I'll call your mother, you grab your camera," Steven shouted. "If we're lucky, we can snag this guy!"

CHAPTER ELEVEN

There were dozens of them—four-by-six-inch glossy photos of the condor that had landed in the parking lot. Magnificent as the condor was—and some photos of him were outstanding, especially the ones where he spread his wings—the people who gathered around the table in the ranger operations office weren't interested in the bird. Or in great photography. Instead, they closely examined the backgrounds of the photos, looking for license plates.

"Don't worry about the out-of-state plates, just check the Arizona ones. Thornton Rawlings' vehicle is registered in this state," said Mike McGinnis. Mike had led the Search and Rescue Team that raised Olivia from the brink. Peering over the top of his glasses, he told Jack, "Look for the letters CIF, followed by the numbers 1003. Here, I wrote it down."

"The more eyes that go over this, the better," Ted

Kenton agreed. "There's a lot of plates showing up in these photos. If you have even the tail-end of a number or letter, set it aside and let Mike or me take a look. Understand?"

"Got it," Jack answered. He felt pretty important being included in this tracking process. It was true that Morgan had found the person who'd sent the e-mail, but now Jack's photographs might tie the man to the scene of the crime.

"We'll give you anything that's questionable," Steven said, nodding. Using a strong magnifying glass, he carefully examined each picture. Studied by someone like Steven, who as a professional photographer really knew how to read them, the pictures could reveal a lot.

"Morgan, would you like to help?" Steven asked him. "You've got some good eyes in your head."

"Sure, Mr. Landon. Nothing would give me more pleasure than to catch this jerk. We're checking only the Arizona plates, right?"

"For starters. Then, if we don't get a hit, we'll enter all the plates into the computer and see if we can find a connection. He could have borrowed a car or rented one—there're a lot of possibilities," Mike said. "Let's hope it's easy."

Jack quickly realized the job was harder than he thought it would be. Many of the plates were out of focus and unreadable, or half-hidden by visitors' legs or the condor's wings. Still, Jack had done exactly what his father had told him to—he'd shot a lot of pictures in rapid-fire succession, hoping that at least one of them would be truly great. It was the sheer volume that made the difference. Less than 20 minutes had passed before Mike called out, "I got it—a perfect match! Right here on the black pickup truck. Looks like your friend Thornton Rawlings happened to be in the park when Olivia was pushed over the edge. Or it least his vehicle was in the parking lot. I guess there's a remote possibility that someone else drove it here."

Jack didn't know how he felt when he heard that news: Relief that this was going to be easier than he'd expected; hatred for Thornton Rawlings; impatience to lock him up so he couldn't hurt anyone else.

"Run a check on the guy," Ted told Mike. "See if he has any criminal history."

"Uh…." Mike turned toward Steven and the boys. "I can't run a check while you three are in here. It's a matter of protecting the privacy of the names on these police records. If you wait outside, I'll let you know if we come up with anything."

"Sure." Jack, his dad, and Morgan went into the hall where they found a soft drink machine. It sold 16-ounce bottles for 75 cents each.

"What a bargain!" Jack exclaimed. Steven put in three one-dollar bills and let the boys punch the buttons for what they wanted. After the change rolled into the coin slot and the drinks rolled down into their waiting hands, the three of them solemnly uncapped the bottles and clinked them together, although the plastic bottles didn't really "clink." "Here's to a great team," Jack said, raising his ginger ale in a toast. "The mighty crime-busters: Morgan, Jack, and Dad."

It wasn't long before Ted came out of the dispatch office. "Thornton Rawlings has a criminal history, all right, for refusing to pay taxes, for disrupting public meetings, for about a hundred unpaid parking tickets, gun violations, and—most serious—for threatening a police officer with a rifle. Seems this fellow thinks government is his number one enemy."

"Wow!" Jack exclaimed. "You know, when Mom was interviewed on CNN, she said she wanted a new law that would make hunters use lead-free ammunition for hunting. Remember? She wanted big fines for anyone who was caught using lead. Do you think that could have set Rawlings off?"

"Anything's possible. I will tell you this: In my experience, it doesn't take very much to beam these conspiracy-types into orbit. Rawlings has been confined to a mental institution on two separate occasions. He suffers from—it says here—" He glanced at a paper in his hand. "From paranoia and delusions of persecution. Your mother's statements might very well have sent him over the edge."

All of them were silent, taking it in. Then Morgan blurted, "So he really *is* a crazy."

"Yeah, but you know...." Thoughtfully, Ted scratched his chin with the edge of the paper. "In spite of all this, all the evidence we have is circumstantial. The twig Rex found was clean, so that didn't help. None of this will be enough to convict him of trying to kill your mother. Not without an eyewitness, or something else that directly links him to the crime."

Morgan asked, "You mean with all that evidence, they won't even throw him in jail? That really stinks!"

Like an alarm going off, Morgan's words reminded Jack of what Ashley had said the night before. The smell! "Mom said she smelled something when the guy came up behind her. Could that be important?"

"What kind of smell?"

"I don't know...." Jack searched his memory. "Like kerosene! She said before she was hit, she smelled it! If we could tie that to Rawlings...."

"How?" Morgan asked. "By visiting his house and sniffing him?"

Ted's voice was suddenly brisk. "Let me grab Mike and check on something. Wait here."

Jack, Morgan, and Steven looked at each other, wondering what Ted would bring back. Moments later, he emerged from an office with Mike, who was holding a printout. "Here's the report on the leather jacket Olivia Landon was wearing," Mike announced. "It says there was a partial handprint on the back of it, but it was unreadable." Mike flipped through the pages. "Looks like the lab technician found gun oil in the handprint."

Morgan's face broke into a slow smile. "Oil? Then, gentlemen, I'd say you've got him."

Ted gave Morgan a quizzical look. "I don't follow."

"You might not be aware of a new technique called AFIS—Automated Fingerprint Identification System. It allows prints to be lifted off of things like human skin and eyeballs. It works when regular print identification fails. Call your Arizona crime unit—they'll tell you."

"Is that true?" Mike asked Steven.

Steven shrugged. "All I know is Morgan is a really smart guy. I believe him."

"Look, I'm telling you, I've read all about it. The oil is dense enough that it will be easy to read with a laser. You just need to send the coat along with Rawlings' fingerprints. If it's him, you'll get a match. And I *know* it's him!"

Ted and Mike exchanged glances. "Let's call up the crime lab and see what they can do for us. You must read true crime stories, kid."

"Me? Only if they're on the Internet."

Steven put his hands on the shoulders of both boys and said, "We're not needed here anymore. Let's go get your mother."

This time Morgan didn't answer, "She's not my mother." He just said, "Lead the way."

When they reached the clinic, they found Olivia waiting, dressed in clean clothes Steven had brought from the lodge. "We have news for you—" Jack began.

"And *we* have news for *you!*" Ashley interrupted. "You should hear what Mom figured out. She's so smart!"

Olivia smiled, saying, "Well, I think that knock on the head might have started my brain spinning in a new direction. I've got an idea why the condors have different-size lead pellets in their intestinal tracts."

"Why, Mom?" Jack asked, amazed that two mysteries could be solved in the same day.

Olivia stood with her hand on the door frame, as though she still felt a bit unsteady from her injuries. "It was Morgan's friend Snipe who gave me the answer. I had a hunch, so I asked if I could use the hospital's computer. I found Snipe's Web site and e-mailed him, and he e-mailed me right back. Of course, we disagree vehemently about the hunt, but I must say other than that, he really is a very nice young man."

Morgan shot Olivia a smile, which she returned. "Snipe explained that the Cash-for-Carcasses hunters usually go after coyotes, since there's so many of them and they're a lot easier to kill than the bigger game. The hunters ride in their pickups with a special whistle that calls coyotes. When the poor animals are within range, they blast them with their shotguns."

"Wait—don't the hunters use rifles?" Morgan asked.

Olivia shook her head no. "Snipe said a rifle bullet can travel more than a mile. If the hunters are shooting from the road, they don't want to risk hitting humans.

Shotgun pellets are accurate only to about 30 yards."

"They don't seem too worried about the coyotes," Jack snapped.

"I know. The whole thing is disgusting, but it's what they do. So the hunters kill the coyotes, then haul the bodies to a Cash-for-Carcasses checkpoint where they get their points tallied. Snipe said there are hundreds of coyote carcasses brought into those places."

"I still don't get it," Jack told her. "What does that have to do with the condors?"

"If I'm right, it means everything." She took a deep breath and said, "Even though the location of these dumping sites is kept pretty quiet, Snipe checked around for me. Guys, there's a checkpoint and dumping site right outside of Tusayan, less than 20 miles from here. There was a hunt three weeks ago. What better place for the condors to congregate than on a huge pile of coyote bodies left out in the woods?"

"Of course!" Steven exclaimed. "It would explain the single source of the lead all the condors fed on!"

Olivia nodded. "Not to mention the different-size pellets. There would have been dozens of different hunters using different weapons. And the dumping site is close enough to the park boundaries that the condors' flight patterns wouldn't have appeared suspicious to people tracking them."

"Which means if you're right, and if they could find the pile and get rid of the lead source—" Steven said, leading Olivia to the glass doors of the clinic's exit.

"Then the condors could be released again!" Ashley finished for him. "And then maybe they could ban the whole stupid hunt altogether!"

"Wouldn't that be something!" Olivia asked, eyes bright.

"I would love to shut down that awful hunt. Imagine, saving the condors *and* the predators. It couldn't get much sweeter."

The five of them walked through the parking lot to the car, moving slowly for Olivia's sake. Morgan gingerly helped Olivia settle herself into the front seat. Then, very carefully because her head still hurt, she turned to face the kids in the backseat. "That's my news. So what's yours?"

"Oh," Jack said casually, "just that we figured out who pushed you over the edge."

CHAPTER TWELVE

As they drove up the rutted, back-country road, Jack noticed how the scenery had muted into autumn browns—dried grasses and dusty junipers ringed by tiny cactus marching into the distance. He watched with satisfaction as his mother carefully stepped out of Shawn's SUV, with Ashley close behind. Although his mother's face was still marred with bruises, she seemed to be brimming with energy.

"I guess this is the end of the line. Now we walk," Steven told Jack and Morgan. "It's only been three days since Olivia got out of the clinic. I sure hope she can handle the hike to the release pen."

"She'll be fine," Jack told him. "She wouldn't miss this for anything, and she told me she looks worse than she feels."

"I'm sure you're right. You've got your camera?"

"Of course I've got my camera."

"Morgan? You have my spare camera?"

"Yeah." He patted the Minolta 350 strapped across his chest. "I don't know how great a photographer I'll be, but I guess I'll give it a try."

"That's the spirit," Steven said, punching Morgan's shoulder in camaraderie. "Let's go."

It was chilly enough for Jack to be able to see his breath as the six of them began to hike their way toward the release point. Far below, a herd of deer munched lazily, raising their heads one by one to look up the mountainside. Sensing no danger, the deer dropped back to the business of eating. Their racks bobbed like driftwood on water.

"How far did you say this is?" Morgan puffed.

"Another eighth of a mile," Shawn called over his shoulder. "It's not too far."

"It's not the distance that's getting to me—it's the fact we're going straight up." Morgan took a deep breath and added, "I need to get in shape."

"That's OK, I'll walk with you, Morgan," Olivia said, dropping back to join him. "I wanted to talk to you for a minute, anyway." Steven quickly caught up with Shawn, and soon the two men gained a substantial lead ahead of the rest of the group. Shawn's red hair gleamed copper in the sun.

Slowing her pace—whether for Morgan's benefit or her own—Olivia walked shoulder to shoulder with him while Jack and Ashley followed. "First things first: The police called. They were able to get a match on Rawlings' partial print, thanks to the information you gave them. I'm supposed to convey their thanks."

Morgan flushed, but kept his eyes straight ahead on the path in front of him. "Well, I'm just glad they got him. I think Rawlings is deranged. He needs help."

"Ms. Lopez was mighty impressed with all you did, I can tell you that."

Morgan stopped walking. "You called Ms. Lopez?" he asked, staring at Olivia as she nodded. "What did she say?"

"Among other things, she said it must have been hard for you to be blamed for something you didn't do. There's a lot of power in words, Morgan."

"Ms. Lopez said that?"

"No. That part comes from me." For a moment, Olivia searched Morgan's face. "I want you to know that I saw the 'sent message' file on my laptop screen. Nine e-mails posted in the middle of the night went out, all without my permission. Why?"

Morgan flushed and studied the ground. "Did you read them?"

"No. I thought about it, but then I decided I should talk to you instead. I want you to explain why you're back to breaking the rules I laid out concerning the use of my laptop and the Internet. What's going on?"

Morgan shrugged. He moved a rock with the toe

of his sneaker, forward, then back, until it formed a groove in the dirt.

"Morgan shouldn't have to tell us anything he doesn't want to," Ashley said defensively. "I trust him. I mean I didn't, but then, I do, I mean *now* I do," she stammered as two round splotches spread across her cheeks. "Shouldn't we believe in him after all he's done for us?"

"Of course," Olivia agreed, "but the fact remains that he sneaked my laptop again and—"

"I wrote the people in Dry Creek," Morgan blurted.

Incredulous, Jack asked, "You *what?*"

"I sent an apology to all the people I'd dissed on my Web site." Shifting uncomfortably, Morgan went on, "I still totally believe in freedom of speech, but...some things have changed. So, I apologized. Why are you all looking at me like that?"

"Did anyone write back?" Jack asked.

"Were there any messages for me, Dr. Landon?"

Olivia shook her head no.

"Maybe they all saw my name and hit the delete key. In a way, it doesn't matter." Narrowing his eyes, he said, "And if you don't believe me, you can read every one of the e-mails I sent. Go ahead and read them. I'm telling you the truth!"

"No, I believe you," Olivia assured him. She put her arm around Morgan, pulling him close. "I think what you did was wonderful. *You're* wonderful."

Immediately Morgan extracted himself from her embrace. "We need to get going. Shawn and Mr. Landon are already way up ahead."

"You think you can go fast enough?" Jack teased.

"Yeah, Morgan, you're wheezing pretty hard," Ashley chimed in. "Can you make it?"

Pulling himself up to full height, Morgan began to move quickly up the path. "Just watch me."

They finally reached the wide plateau at the top of the cliffs. Steven and Shawn were deep in discussion, their hands punctuating the air as they talked. Looking up, Steven cried, "Hey, what took you so long?"

"Nothing, we were just talking to our friend," Ashley called back.

Shawn hoisted his pack onto his shoulder. "I was telling Steven how they found enough lead shot at the dump site to poison a thousand birds. We burned what was left of the carcasses and then buried the ashes. The condors won't be back there."

"What about other dump sites?" Jack demanded. "Couldn't this whole thing happen all over again?"

"The Cash-for-Carcasses folks said they'd be sure to keep any future dump site at least 100 miles from the Grand Canyon. They were pretty shook up when I told them what had happened."

"I still hate the hunt," Ashley said, shaking her head.

"Me, too. But Cash-for-Carcasses said they'd work with us, and that's a start. You ready, Olivia?"

"Absolutely!"

Inside the cover of the green mesh netting, Steven set up his tripod. "Better attach your telephoto lens," he instructed Jack. "And be alert. When that condor soars, you need to sweep your camera along its path and shoot as fast as you can. Don't try to conserve film. Just aim and shoot. You too, Morgan."

"I could work this a lot better if it had a joystick," Morgan said, fooling with the focus.

"This is better than computers. This is life. Look sharp—you don't want to miss the launch."

As he had the time before, Jack used his camera lens to track what was happening in the flight pen. When Shawn and Olivia approached, 87 stepped back, its bright eyes lit with curiosity.

"Stay alert," Steven said. "Shawn's starting to move."

Shawn had left the pen to walk through the low scrub juniper trees toward the edge of the cliff. Olivia was right behind him.

"Get ready," Steven told Jack.

Jack wasn't sure what to expect—would Shawn throw the bird into the air? Instead, Shawn set him down about 20 feet from the edge.

Number 87 looked around, then back toward Shawn as if asking his permission. In an instant he started to run—to run, not fly!—like a high jumper gathering momentum. When he reached the edge of the cliff, his wide, outstretched wings caught the air current and off he went! The takeoff was so spectacular that Jack lowered his camera; he wanted to see this with his own eyes, not through a lens.

Four feet long from beak to tip of tail, his black body feathers catching the sun, his massive wings curving like parentheses joined in the middle, Condor 87 looked breathtaking. With the feathers at the end of each wing spread out like eight giant fingers, his wingspan reached nine feet from tip to tip. The white lining of the wings' undersides was clearly visible as he climbed and soared. By the time Jack remembered that he was supposed to be taking pictures, Condor 87 had flown too far for even Jack's telephoto to capture.

"Wasn't that—?" Jack couldn't find a word powerful enough to describe what he'd just seen.

"Cool," Morgan said, nodding. "It was as good as the very best graphics on my computer—maybe even better." Raising his fist into the air, Morgan shouted, "Nature rules!"

AFTERWORD

Here I sit on the rim of the most well-known canyon in the world. Peering down 5,000 feet into the main stem of the Colorado, I view a river running red and brown and muddy from spring snowmelt high in the Rocky Mountains of Colorado. Crystal-blue skies signal the return of what is fast becoming the annual spring and summer wildlife event in northern Arizona—a must-see for tourists and residents alike. Looking up, I see the blue sky darken as though there has been a sudden, momentary eclipse of the sun. The California condor, gliding on its huge wings, is returning to the South Rim of Grand Canyon National Park.

With its prehistoric appearance, the condor brings goose bumps to my arms and tears to my eyes. This marvel in the sky is a salute to the effectiveness of the Endangered Species Act and a reward to the many biologists and administrators who have toiled over efforts to reintroduce this bird into its natural habitat. *Gymnogyps californianus*—a member of the vulture family that scavenged on mastodons, camels, and bison as it evolved over much of the last ten million years— once soared over a range that extended from Canada to Mexico. By the early 1900s, the California condor had become extremely rare as a result of human activities. Most had been shot or had died from feeding on carcasses contaminated by lead shot, pesticides, or other poisons. To save the condor, biologists started a captive breeding program with birds they removed from the wild. Thanks to that program there are now 185 condors in the world. To date, 59 have been reintroduced to their former habitats in California and Arizona. The rest live in breeding facilities. But California condors are not out of the woods yet.

In *Over the Edge,* Gloria Skurzynski and Alane Ferguson create an adventure that is based on more fact than fiction. Unfortunately, humankind continues to ignore lessons from the past. In summer 2000, lead poisoning was the confirmed cause of death for three condors and the suspected killer of two others. This was the worst incidence of condor deaths since the birds were reintroduced into the park in 1996. Within the park and the vast expanses of the surrounding Colorado Plateau, condors feed primarily on deer, elk, and bighorn sheep. During the hunting season, the carcasses of game animals that escape and later die of their wounds are scavenged upon, lead bullets and all. Lead-ridden intestines in gut piles left by hunters throughout the forest pose a potential risk, as do the carcasses left by poachers and by varmint hunters—people who kill any and all predators for sport and money. Although hunting is illegal within the park, there is no way to keep the birds from flying beyond its protective boundaries.

There are other human-related threats to the condor's survival. Power poles and lines can electrocute birds that perch on or fly into them. This is why we are in the process of outfitting these lines with devices that will make them "raptor proof." A more difficult problem is dealing with the birds' natural curiosity. Some birds are attracted to overlooks and buildings frequented by the more than five million people who visit the park each year. Although feeding the birds is strictly prohibited, some people still offer them food. They forget that these birds are wild animals capable of snapping off fingers or tearing out huge chunks of flesh with their powerful beaks. Birds that seem to like to hang out with people are recaptured and returned to The Peregrine Fund facility for a little more "growing up" time.

The employment of devices that use satellites to track condors promises to be a giant step toward our goal of making the environment safe for these birds. As you learned in the story, condors in the park currently are fitted with radio tags. Satellite tracking provides a record of each bird's daily activities—where it flies, roosts, feeds, and perches. The Peregrine Fund has purchased four of these devices. Eventually, we hope to have one for each condor.

In spring 2001, condors came one step closer to recovery. A single egg was laid in a cave on a steep cliff in a remote section of Grand Canyon National Park. But as exciting and hopeful as the wild breeding of a species once on the brink of extinction can be, it does not guarantee success. It will not be until we, the human species, ban or severely restrict the use of lead in hunting and fishing, express our disgust to state legislators over the continued obliteration of predators through varmint hunts, and urge our federal representatives to enforce environmental protection laws that condors and other endangered species will have a chance to truly recover. When we as humans achieve these goals so that species no longer fall victim to humankind, then we will have indeed achieved a notable victory.

Elaine F. Leslie
Wildlife Biologist
Grand Canyon National Park

DON'T MISS—

WOLF STALKER
MYSTERY #1
Fast-paced adventure has the Landons on the trail
of an injured wolf in Yellowstone National Park.

CLIFF-HANGER
MYSTERY #2
Jack's desire to help the headstrong Lucky Deal
brings him face-to-face with a hungry cougar in
Mesa Verde National Park.

DEADLY WATERS
MYSTERY #3
Jack and Ashley's efforts to save an injured manatee
involve them in a thrilling chase through the Everglades.

RAGE OF FIRE
MYSTERY #4
In this tale of myth and mystery, a Vietnamese orphan named
Danny leads Ashley and Jack into a steaming volcano in
Hawaii Volcanoes National Park.

THE HUNTED
MYSTERY #5
While attempting to help a young Mexican runaway, Jack and
Ashley flee for their lives from an enraged mother grizzly in
Glacier National Park.

GHOST HORSES
MYSTERY #6
Life-threatening accidents plague the Landons as they investigate the mysterious deaths of some white mustangs on a trip
to Zion National Park.

COMING SOON—

VALLEY OF DEATH
MYSTERY #8

ABOUT THE AUTHORS

An award-winning mystery writer and an award-winning science writer—who are also mother and daughter—are working together on Mysteries in Our National Parks!

Alane (Lanie) Ferguson's first mystery, *Show Me the Evidence,* won the Edgar Award, given by the Mystery Writers of America.

Gloria Skurzynski's *Almost the Real Thing* won the American Institute of Physics Science Writing Award.

Lanie lives in Elizabeth, Colorado. Gloria lives in Salt Lake City, Utah. To work together on a novel, they connect by phone, fax, and e-mail and "often forget which one of us wrote a particular line."

Gloria's e-mail: gloriabooks@qwest.net
Her Web site: http://gloriabooks.com
Lanie's e-mail: aferguson@sprynet.com